As if there were no one in there . . .

Cassidy came to a halt as she saw what was idling a few feet away. The black Trans Am with the tinted glass. It gave her a weird feeling to glance at the window and see nothing but darkness, as if there were no one in there, no one at all.

Impulsively, she rapped on the dark glass of the driver's window. Nothing happened.

She rapped again, more insistently this time. Still no response.

Shrugging, she turned away from the car and began to walk.

But as she moved, so did the car.

It moved slowly, quietly, inching forward almost imperceptibly, keeping pace with Cassidy's steps.

She stepped back, away from the car.

It stopped moving, its engine still murmuring quietly.

What kind of game was he playing?

Terrifying thrillers by Diane Hoh:

Funhouse
The Accident
The Invitation
The Train
The Fever

Nightmare Hall: The Silent Scream
Nightmare Hall: The Roommate
Nightmare Hall: Deadly Attraction
Nightmare Hall: The Wish
Nightmare Hall: The Scream Team
Nightmare Hall: Guilty
Nightmare Hall: Pretty Please
Nightmare Hall: The Experiment
Nightmare Hall: The Night Walker
Nightmare Hall: Sorority Sister
Nightmare Hall: Last Date
Nightmare Hall: The Whisperer
Nightmare Hall: Monster
Nightmare Hall: The Initiation
Nightmare Hall: Truth or Die
Nightmare Hall: Book of Horrors
Nightmare Hall: Last Breath

NIGHTMARE HALL

Last Breath

DIANE HOH

SCHOLASTIC INC.
New York Toronto London Auckland Sydney

ISBN 0-590-48648-9

Copyright © 1994 Diane Hoh.
All rights reserved. Published by Scholastic Inc.

12 11 10 9 8 7 6 5 4 3 2   4 5 6 7 8 9/9

Printed in the U.S.A.   01

First Scholastic printing, November 1994

NIGHTMARE HALL

Last Breath

Scholastic Corporation / Bantam / Hippocampus books

Prologue

Arms are important. They reach for things, they hug, they lift and carry, they perform tasks, they wave hello and good-bye.

Legs are important. They move a body from place to place, they pedal, they drive a car, they dance, they jog, they kick a football, they jump.

A mouth talks, eats, drinks, kisses, argues, smiles.

A nose sneezes and smells roses and cabbage.

Ears hear music and conversation and bells and train whistles and babies crying.

Eyes see things, cry, wink. Eyes reflect the soul.

But it is the mind that matters most. When the mind is lost, all is lost.

A mind is a terrible thing to lose.

Chapter 1

Suite 56A of the Quad, a huge, multiplex dorm on the campus of Salem University, was bustling with activity in the early morning hours of a chilly day in late fall. Four people were trying to get dressed for classes at the same time, darting in and out of closets, waving hair dryers around like weapons, jockeying for positions at mirrors to expertly or haphazardly apply makeup. Beds were unmade, books and notebooks were scattered among the bedding, clothes lay like anthills on the floor, and the tenants ran from one of the two small rooms to the other through the tiny half-bath that joined the two as music played loudly over the chaos.

"Now that you're back among the living," Talia Quick, a tall, pretty girl with clear, glowing skin and long, shiny yellow-gold hair, said to Cassidy Kirk, "does that mean we can't borrow your clothes anymore?"

Cassidy, brushing her own thick, red, shoulder-length hair, laughed. "Talia, the only thing of mine that would fit *you* is a scarf. I'm a munchkin, you and Ann are Vikings. I wish I could say the same for Sophie! I haven't seen my red sweater since she borrowed it when I first got sick, and Sophie never, *ever* hangs anything up. She has blouses of mine that are lying in the bottom of the closet, looking like an elephant danced on them."

"I'll iron them," Sophie Green said, overhearing as she came into the room Cassidy shared with Ann Ataska. "I promise." Sophie was small and rounded, with eyes as dark as chestnuts. Velcro rollers dotted her dark hair. "The very first chance I get."

"Which will be never," Cassidy said drily. "I've known you for three months, Sophie Green, and I have never once seen you with an iron in your hand. Do you even own one?"

"Well, actually, no," Sophie admitted, heedlessly ripping the rollers from her hair and dropping them on the dresser. "But I could always borrow one, couldn't I?"

"You could. But you won't." Cassidy slipped into a blue denim shirt. "Never mind, Sophie.

I'm just so glad to be out of that bed and feeling normal again."

A severe asthma attack had felled Cassidy, sending her to the infirmary briefly, and then back to her own bed for three days.

"You were run-down," the doctor had told her before she was discharged. "That's why it hit you so hard. You're doing too much. Take it easy. Life is too short to race through it."

Well, maybe. But who decided what was "doing too much"? Cassidy *liked* being busy. College was fun, and there were a million things to do: classes to attend, clubs to join, activities to take part in, parties, dances, movies to see. It was hard to pack everything in.

Chronic asthma had kept Cassidy out of things as a child. Later, when new medication controlled her condition effectively, she found to her disappointment that the most exciting thing to do on a Saturday night in her rural community was drive into town and watch the grass in the park grow. Talleyrand, Virginia, didn't even have a movie theater.

Salem campus, on the other hand, was a festival of fun things to do.

So being sick this time had been a drag. Maybe she would take it just a tiny bit easier. At first, anyway. Three days in bed with her inhaler, the tube of medication which she could inhale, enabling her to get through severe asthma attacks, had left her feeling as if she'd been riding a roller coaster nonstop for hours.

But her friends had been great about keeping her up-to-date on class assignments, so she was at least basically caught up.

Ann Ataska, her pale hair caught up in a sleek, smooth French twist, came into the room carrying a pile of books. "Psych is really driving me nuts, if you'll excuse the pun," she said. "Maybe I've picked the wrong field."

All four girls were planning to major in psychology, perhaps because they all had at least one relative working successfully in the field. Ann's father was a psychiatric social worker, Sophie's mother and Cassidy's aunt were psychiatric nurses, and Talia's mother was a psychiatrist in a well-known psychiatric facility in Albany.

Tapping one long, scarlet-tipped fingernail on a framed picture sitting on Cassidy's dresser, Ann said, "Trav's been asking me about you. I didn't notice him visiting while you were sick, though. Did he call?"

"No." Cassidy looked at the picture. Dark, moody eyes looked out at her from the frame. Why hadn't she put the picture away, or given it back to Travis? He could give it to some girl who was prepared to drop everything and make Travis McVey the center of her universe, devoting herself totally and completely to him. Unlike Cassidy Kirk, who insisted on having a life of her own. A very *busy* life of her own.

She had tried to explain to Travis what it was like, growing up with asthma. The medications then hadn't been as effective and she'd spent way too much time lying in bed, missing out on things, feeling "different" from other kids. Now, she had medication that kept things under control and she took it faithfully, knowing that without it, she couldn't live a completely normal life. Sometimes it wasn't enough, like with this latest attack. But most of the time, it worked.

Maybe she *did* work too hard at convincing herself and everyone around her that she was, now, strong and healthy. It was so important to her. She had thought Travis understood.

He hadn't.

"But Sawyer came to see me," she told Ann defiantly. "Brought me violets, too. And a package of cinnamon gum. He knows I love it." Sawyer Duncan, one of the most popular boys on campus, was as busy as she was. Unlike Travis, a tall and bony farm boy, Sawyer was big and solid and comfortingly easygoing. He understood what it was to live an active social life at school. Much easier to deal with than

7

Travis, who accused her of "chasing herself" with such a busy schedule. "I'm surprised you leave time to breathe," he'd said caustically when they'd had that last, awful argument.

Two days later, she'd remembered that remark when steel-like bands of pain had fastened themselves around her chest, and every breath she struggled to take was agony. The inhaler hadn't helped, and she'd ended up, briefly, in the infirmary.

Maybe Trav and the doctor were right. She should schedule in some time to relax. Stress made the asthma worse, she already knew that. Easing up on her schedule was probably a good idea.

But she couldn't ease up *this* week. Too much to do. Maybe next week?

"Come on, you guys, hurry up!" Cassidy urged. "I don't want to be late for Bruin's class my first day back." Psychology 101 Professor Leona Bruin was one of the strictest teachers at Salem. Her reputation was well-known, and they had all groaned when they had drawn her as a teacher. Talia adored her, saying Bruin reminded her of her mother. "Strong and smart," she said admiringly. The guys in class mostly hated Bruin, and Ann and Sophie were scared to death of her. Cassidy had found her to be fair. Strict, but fair.

"I feel like I've just been let out of prison," she said as they hurried across Salem's beautiful, rolling campus in the early-morning sunshine. The huge old trees lining the stone walkways had already turned color, and were beginning to drop their leaves. "Isn't it a gorgeous day? The air feels fantastic!"

Ann, who was from Florida, shrugged and burrowed deeper in her heavy cable-knit sweater. "Too cold! This is only November. Feels like February to me."

"You'd better toughen up, surfer-girl," Talia warned. "The worst is yet to come. Anyway, the cold puts color in our cheeks, and that's what Cassidy needs."

Cassidy hastily rubbed both cheeks with the palms of her hands. If there was one thing she didn't want to do, it was walk into psych class looking pale and wan. If Travis was already seated, he'd take one look at her and think she was pining away because of *him*. Which she wasn't.

Travis was there. But he didn't look up when the quartet from the Quad walked in. He was doodling aimlessly on a piece of paper and kept his dark, curly head down.

On purpose, Cassidy thought as she took her seat. He's ignoring me on purpose. Like I care.

Still, it did sting, a little. She'd been away

from classes for three days. And he hadn't once called or come to see her. Okay, he'd asked Ann about her. Big deal.

They had dated steadily for three months. Then . . . the fight. A big fight. World War III, both of them shouting and yelling. It was disgusting. But he could have come to the Quad to see if she was still among the living. Wouldn't have killed him.

Sawyer, sitting off to her left, sent her a wave and a smile.

She flashed him a brilliant grin, wishing Travis would lift his head and see it.

He didn't.

But it wasn't because of Travis that Cassidy had trouble concentrating in class. The asthma attack, the only one she'd had since arriving on campus, had drained her, and although she was anxious to get back in gear, she had to admit she wasn't feeling one hundred percent yet. A leftover headache plagued her off and on, and she wouldn't have minded having one more day off to sleep. But she'd missed so much class time already, and there were things to do this weekend. Important things. Life had been going on without her all this time. She *hated* that!

She struggled to pay attention to Professor Bruin's lecture. Something about the fragility of the human mind. Not very interesting. Unless, of course, you happened to have a fragile mind. Cassidy didn't. It was only her lungs that could use some strengthening.

"Ms. Kirk, may I see you after class, please?"

Cassidy's head snapped up. She was horrified to discover that she'd actually been dozing, head down, eyes closed. That had never happened before. The girl sitting opposite her snickered. Cassidy silenced her with a look designed to melt steel. But she listened attentively to every one of Professor Bruin's remaining words.

She had seldom been so happy to see a class end.

"Ms. Kirk," the teacher said when Cassidy was standing before her, "about the essay on the fragility of the mind. When do you expect to turn that in?"

The essay had been assigned two weeks before the attack had taken Cassidy out. She frowned. "I did turn that in, Professor Bruin! What I mean is, I finished that paper before I got sick. I gave it to a friend to turn in. Didn't you get it?"

"Well, now, I wouldn't be asking you for it if I had, would I?"

Cassidy thought for a moment. She had finished the paper and given it to Travis *before* their relationship self-destructed. In fact, the argument had begun because she was cutting psych class to finish making plans for a car wash the freshmen psych majors were holding. A fund-raiser, the money would then be used to hold a dance, also a fund-raiser. The money from the dance was to go to the mental health clinic in Twin Falls, Salem's host community. The plans were late. She just hadn't had time to get to them, and since she'd finished the essay on time, she'd decided to simply cut class. There were only so many hours in a day.

Travis had grudgingly agreed to turn in the paper for her. She thought now that he'd stuck it into his backpack. Hadn't he? But then he'd accused her of having her "priorities screwed-up" and told her to get someone else to finish the car wash arrangements. "You're not indispensable!" he had said, his voice cool. "Why is it so important to you to think that you are?"

Later that day, they'd resumed the argument and taken it to its logical conclusion . . . an angry good-bye.

But she had assumed that he'd turned in the paper first. *Before* that last blowup.

"I'll check it out," she promised the psych professor. "I did finish that paper. All I have to do is find it."

She went looking for Travis, anger bubbling in her chest as she hurried to Lester, a tall, skinny, brick dorm opposite the Quad. He hadn't turned the paper in? Had he just forgotten about it? They'd both been upset. It could have slipped his mind when he got into the psych room. So it could still be in his backpack. She'd get it from him, turn it in, and Dr. Bruin would know that she actually had finished the assignment.

"What paper?" Travis said when she explained why she was there.

He didn't look all that happy to see her, it seemed to Cassidy. She'd sent someone looking for him and when he came out of the elevator and saw her standing in the lobby, he didn't smile.

His eyes used to light up when he saw me, she thought, feeling a pang of regret as he approached. But he had wanted too much from her, too much time, too much devotion.

Maybe that was irritation she was feeling, not regret.

"I don't remember your giving me any paper," he added when she had reminded him.

"But I did, Trav! I can't believe you don't remember. We were standing outside of the Quad, near the fountain. I had the car wash to set up, so I decided to cut psych, remember?"

Her lips tightened. "You gave me a lecture. But you did take the paper. I think you put it in your backpack."

His eyes were uncomprehending. "Well, I'll go look. But I'd have run across it by now if it was in there." He took the stairs two at a time. He was an athlete. A runner and a biker. She had planned to go to his track meets, his bicycle races, cheering him on. But not now. He wouldn't want her there.

He was back in minutes, the black backpack dangling from his hands. "You look for it," he said. "You'll recognize it faster than I would."

The paper wasn't there. The backpack was stuffed to overflowing with notebooks, looseleaf, paperbacks, a wallet, sunglasses, but no essay with Cassidy's name on it.

"Maybe you just thought you gave it to me," he said as she straightened up with a disappointed sigh. "Seems to me you had a lot on your mind that day." Without smiling, he added, "But then, when don't you?"

"Please, Travis, don't start," she said, trying to concentrate on that day, trying to remember. Could he be right? Maybe she'd intended to give it to him, and then forgotten. She'd been thinking about the car wash. So much to do, so little time! Maybe she'd never handed him the paper, after all.

"But if I didn't give it to you," she said, "then where is it? I *know* I finished it."

He shrugged. "In your room, I guess. Anyway," he added stiffly as he bent to refasten his backpack, "is that all you wanted?"

Images flashed across Cassidy's mind: The two of them meeting for the first time at a bike club gathering. A few nights later, dancing together for hours in the rec center. Walking across campus holding hands and talking nonstop about school and how different it was from high school. Sitting in a darkened movie theater sharing a giant box of popcorn and laughing at Bill Murray's antics. Biking together to the nearby state park. Sitting in Travis's car, kissing, his arms feeling so right, so right.

But she'd been so busy, working like mad to prove just how strong and healthy she really was now. And after a while, he had said, "You never have any time for me. You fill up every minute with activities and you don't leave any time for *us*."

She shook the images away. Life was too short for regret.

"Yes," she said clearly, "the paper was all I wanted. I'm going to go hunt for it in my room."

"Good luck," he said as she turned away and hurried from Lester.

She searched every inch of her cluttered

dorm room and when Ann, Talia, and Sophie came home, she enlisted their aid, too. They lifted clothing from chairs and beds, set aside towers of books on shelves and tables, even slipped their CD's from holders thinking the paper might have slipped down behind the wooden racks. It hadn't.

Although Cassidy was absolutely positive that she had slaved over and finished the essay for psych 101 class, the paper was nowhere to be found.

"I'm sure I gave it to Travis," she said when they'd given up and were sitting on the floor trying to restore some semblance of order in the room. "I remember it so clearly. At least, I think I do. But he doesn't have it." One hand went to her aching forehead. "Maybe that stupid asthma attack damaged my brain cells."

"Or maybe," Sophie said lightly, "Travis is madder at you than you thought he was."

Cassidy's eyes went to Sophie's round, pink-cheeked face. "How could he be madder than I thought he was? He was furious."

"My point exactly." Sophie fell silent then, busily sorting CD's, but her implication was clear to Cassidy.

She thinks Travis *has* that paper, Cassidy thought miserably, getting up to go over and lie down on her bed. Or *had* it, anyway. Sophie thinks maybe he deliberately sabotaged me with Dr. Bruin because we had that fight.

It was Ann who came to Travis's defense. "He wouldn't do something so slimy," she said firmly, tossing a handful of sweatshirts into the closet. "Not Travis."

But Cassidy, remembering Travis's face burning with anger on that day of their last argument, wasn't so sure.

Chapter 2

On Saturday morning, the autumn-hued campus was bathed in bright sunshine, but there were dark clouds gathering low on the horizon.

"Let's hope," Cassidy said as she dressed in bright red sweats, "that the rain holds off until after the car wash. We've hustled our buns pulling this together. No one wants to see it washed out."

Ann, plucking her eyebrows at the dresser mirror, laughed at Cassidy's unintentional play on words. Sophie said, "It's not supposed to rain until later. We should rake in a pile of money for the dance. So relax, Cassidy. All of your efforts will not be in vain."

Talia, in exercise clothing, came in, telling Cassidy that she had just talked to her mother on the phone. With an impish grin, she said, "She says you probably lost that essay on purpose. Passive-aggression, she called it. You didn't really want to turn it in, so you lost it instead. Isn't the human mind intriguing? And that'll be fifty bucks, please."

"I'm sure your mother charges more than that," Cassidy said drily.

"Not over the phone."

"Well, I don't *have* fifty bucks, and I *didn't* lose that essay. Travis did." Cassidy wasn't wild about the idea of Talia discussing her with a shrink, even if it was her own mother. And she had, too, wanted to turn in that essay. She'd worked hard on it.

Psychiatry was obviously not an exact science.

None of Cassidy's roommates would be at the car wash. They had helped her set up the event, but Ann was baby-sitting for her economics professor, a widow with three children for whom she often sat, saying she needed the "brownie points" because her grade in that class was "iffy." Talia was running in a race, and Sophie had left an important paper until the last minute, as Sophie always did, and planned to spend the day in the library.

"Traitors!" Cassidy had accused half-seriously. "My own roommates, letting me down. Can't count on anybody these days."

"You'll have tons of people," Sophie assured her. "Everyone I know is planning to help."

Cassidy had no choice but to take Sophie's word for it.

On the way to breakfast in the Quad's basement dining hall, Ann asked Cassidy, "So, is the new love of your life going to be there? At the car wash, I mean."

"Sure. That's how I met him, remember? We put out a call for volunteers, and blond, gorgeous Sawyer Duncan showed up, almost like I'd placed an order."

"And the rest is history," Ann said drily. "Poor Trav."

"I didn't *dump* Travis," Cassidy replied, glancing up at Ann who, like Talia, was considerably taller than her. "We had an argument, that's all."

"You mean a *fight*," Sophie said. "I heard you guys yelling at each other. Sounded like a fight to me."

"Leave Cassidy alone," Talia ordered. "She's been sick. Quit picking on her."

My sentiments exactly, Cassidy thought as they entered an uncrowded dining hall. Leave poor Cassidy alone. She's not quite herself just yet.

Sometime today, between the car wash and the movie Sawyer was taking her to later, she was going to have to rewrite that stupid psych paper. Dr. Bruin had made it very clear that asthma or not, Cassidy Kirk was expected to turn in the assignment.

"You're not eating anything," Sawyer's voice said over her shoulder ten minutes later. He sat down in the chair beside her. His broad bulk, in jeans and a blue windbreaker, filled the chair. His sun-streaked blond hair was windblown, and a grin creased his strong, ruddy face. "Aren't you supposed to be rebuilding your strength? We've got a busy day ahead of us, kiddo."

Cassidy poked at watery scrambled eggs with her fork. "Nothing on *this* plate is going to rebuild anyone's strength. Anyway, I'm fine. Let's get started before the rain does."

The car wash was being held in the center of campus. Although Cassidy had worried that not enough people would show up, they had plenty of volunteers, anxious to be outside in the sunshine while it lasted. Cassidy decided, after some thought, to ask that only one person work on one car at a time. She suspected that working in groups would cause so much goofing-off with garden hoses and buckets of soapy water, they'd never get done. People who weren't washing cars could keep the lines of cars in order and the car-wash supplies filled up.

No one complained about working solo.

"This place is a madhouse!" Sawyer, pail in hand, declared as he brushed past Cassidy an hour later. "More people than cars."

"We'll just get done faster this way," Cassidy answered. She was scrubbing the white sidewalls of a blue convertible, using a scouring pad. "And I'll get out of here in time to work on my psych paper."

"The one you lost?"

I didn't *lose* it! Cassidy thought, irritated. But Sawyer was already on his way to the next waiting car.

The line didn't seem to get any shorter. As sparkling clean vehicles pulled away, dirty ones sprouted like mushrooms in their places. Seeing the apparently endless line circling the parking lot like a wagon train, Cassidy sighed. That psych paper might have to wait until tomorrow.

In spite of her impatience, she couldn't help admiring the black TransAm when it pulled up in front of her. Through a thick layer of dust and grime, she could see its clean, sporty lines, imagine it roaring up the highway between Salem University and the nearby town of Twin Falls. She had no trouble picturing herself behind the wheel.

Impossible to see who really *was* behind the wheel. All the window glass was tinted a dark, smoky color that kept the driver hidden from view. Cassidy didn't recognize the car. A cool car. Whoever owned it was probably a really cool person.

Two red plastic hearts tied together and fastened firmly to the driver's door handle bounced about as Cassidy sprayed the TransAm with one of several garden hoses. Thinking Sawyer would love this car, she glanced around, intending to signal him.

She didn't see him anywhere. And if she called his name, he'd never hear her over this din.

Giving up, Cassidy returned to the task at hand.

When the black TransAm was spotless, the driver rolled the window down a crack and thrust a crisp, ten-dollar bill through the opening. Cassidy caught only a glimpse of a cream-colored parka hood.

She was fumbling in her leather fanny pack for change when the TransAm's engine roared, gears shifted, and it veered out of line to peel across the parking lot, disappearing from sight.

Weird. Ten bucks for a car wash? The guy must be loaded.

There was a brief lull in customers just then and a sudden, chill spray from Sawyer's garden hose on her left ear caught Cassidy by surprise, distracting her from the vanished TransAm with its generous, unseen driver. Using her own hose as a weapon she took up the challenge. Others armed with hoses and buckets joined in. Arcs and streams of water cascaded down upon the already-puddled parking lot, soaking jackets and jeans, hair and hands, faces and feet.

"Enough, enough!" Cassidy finally shouted, her own clothes dripping. "Lay down your arms!" A new line of cars had formed, snaking around the parking lot in a semicircle. "Back to work!"

There were groans at an end to the horseplay, but everyone obeyed.

It was much harder working in wet clothes, Cassidy promptly discovered. The sun had disappeared behind the thickening clouds, turning the air chilly. Her sweats clung to her like tissue paper, and her hands felt like ice. Dumb idea, getting wet, she told herself as she approached the third car in line. I don't have time to get sick again. Dumb, dumb, dumb!

She saw the two red plastic hearts before she noticed the car idling next to her.

The black TransAm.

In line again, and for good reason. Although it had been spotless when it raced from the parking lot twenty minutes or so earlier, it was once again coated with a thick layer of dirt.

Cassidy peered more closely at the car. Couldn't be the same one. That guy had paid ten bucks. He wouldn't have gone right out and gotten the car filthy again so fast, would he?

But there were the red plastic hearts, dangling from the driver's door handle.

What were the chances that there were *two* black TransAms on the campus of Salem University with dark, tinted glass and a pair of red plastic hearts tied to a door handle?

The TransAm honked impatiently.

Cassidy washed the car again. As she moved around it, hose in hand, she thought how eerie the tinted glass made the car look. It gave her a weird feeling to glance at the window and see nothing but darkness, as if there were no one in there, no one at all. Like, she thought as she wiped the hood dry, a futuristic car that drives itself.

Creepy.

It occurred to her as she gave the driver's door one last, quick swipe with her rag, that the car might belong to a benefactor. Someone who wanted them to make tons of money and was willing to go through the car wash repeatedly to help out. And didn't want to take credit for his generosity.

Nice guy.

The window slid open a crack. The bill that slid through the opening was a crisp, new twenty.

"Please wait for your change this time," Cassidy said quickly, delving into the pack at her waist. But her fingers were so cold, they moved slowly. Too slowly.

The TransAm didn't wait.

It was gone in a splash of cold water before Cassidy's fingers had closed around the correct change.

She stared after it for a long time, absentmindedly fingering the crisp twenty.

"Pretty dumb, if you ask me," a voice said from behind her.

Travis. In the same blue plaid flannel shirt and blue windbreaker he'd been wearing the first time she ever saw him. With the same intense expression on his lean, bony face.

Cassidy turned around, zipping her pack closed. "Dumb? Oh, not waiting for his change, you mean? Yeah, I guess it is. I think the guy is just trying to help us out. With a car like that, I suppose he can afford it."

"I wasn't talking about a car," Travis said, his voice as cold as Cassidy's hands. "I didn't see any car. I was talking about someone who just got out of the infirmary fooling around out here in the cold in wet clothes. That's what I meant by dumb."

Cassidy bristled. So he *had* known she was sick. Well, not really *sick*, the way Travis was making it sound. Just an asthma attack. You didn't get those from being soaked on a chilly day. Anyway, if he wasn't going to help with the car wash, he should keep his opinions to himself.

But he never did. Travis had told her he was the first person in his family to go to college. His father had lost the family farm to bad debts, moved to the city and worked in a factory, and died an unhappy man. Travis was determined that wouldn't happen to him. He did go to parties and dances and had joined several groups, but his main purpose in being at Salem was getting a degree.

She had accused him, on that last day, of being too serious, and he had accused her of joining too many activities just to prove a point.

Two opinions that might as well have been left unexpressed.

"A," she said crisply, "I'm not fooling around, I'm washing cars. B, we had a water fight, not that it's any of your business, and C, it *isn't* any of your business." Tossing her hair, which was spiralling into rust-colored corkscrews from being wet, she turned her back on

Travis and moved toward the next car in line, a blue Chevy.

When she glanced over her shoulder a few minutes later, he was gone.

Good. She already *had* a perfectly good father. She wasn't in the market for another one.

Still, Travis had a point. The sky was a dark charcoal-gray now, and the air continued to turn colder. She was freezing.

"Why don't you go back to the Quad?" Sawyer suggested when he joined her during another lull and found her shivering. "Take a nice, hot shower and get into some dry clothes." He smiled down at her. "Can't have you getting sick again."

Why couldn't Travis have said it that nicely, instead of calling her "dumb"?

"I'm okay," she insisted. "I'm running this thing. I can't chicken out while everyone else is still here."

"Sure, you can." Sawyer took off his windbreaker and draped it around her shoulders. "That's *why* you can leave, because there are so many other people here. You don't have to do everything yourself, Cassidy. Haven't you ever heard of delegating responsibility?"

Travis had said almost the same thing, during that last lengthy argument they'd had. Irritated, Cassidy said sharply, "Things are starting to pick up again." She glanced around the parking lot. "Here comes another batch. When this group thins out, I'll go dry off, I promise."

They went back to work.

This time, the black TransAm pulled up to Cassidy so slowly, so quietly, she didn't notice it at first. Busy finishing an old red VW bug, she was backing away from that car, rag in hand, when the backs of her knees collided gently with metal.

She turned to face the familiar black car with its protective window glass.

It was filthy again.

This was ridiculous. Was it a joke? Was he testing her to see if she'd even realize that this was his third car wash of the day? One thing she *was* certain of, it wasn't anyone she *knew*. No one she knew threw money around so carelessly.

She walked around to the driver's side. There they were, two little plastic hearts.

Cassidy hesitated. There was something about the car that raised the hairs on the back of her neck. Maybe it was the eeriness of the dark glass. Or maybe it was the elusiveness of the driver. All of the other drivers rolled down their windows after their wash, joked with their car washer. Maybe talked for a minute, said they were pleased with the job.

Not this guy. He barely cracked the window.

Another impatient honk sounded from the TransAm.

What choice did she have? She couldn't very well rap on the window and say, "I'm sorry, sir, but you've had your two turns today. That's all we allow." Besides, he was *paying*.

And pay he did, this time with another twenty-dollar bill so new, it crackled when he pushed it through a tiny opening in his window.

And although Cassidy scrambled to yank change from her pack, he was gone again before she had it unzipped.

The little red hearts flew, banging against the door as the TransAm raced from the parking lot for the third time.

"That is the weirdest thing!" she murmured, slipping the crisp twenty into her pack. Maybe in the future she'd keep a lookout on campus for the TransAm. Creepy though it was, if she saw it, she should thank their generous benefactor.

By the time the clouds split, sending a torrential downpour across campus, Cassidy was safely back at the Quad, showered, dried, and wrapped in fresh, dry sweats. She was lying on the floor, her head resting on her money-stuffed fanny pack, hand in a bag of microwave popcorn sitting beside her. Ann and Sophie were sitting on the beds, each armed with a hairdryer. Sawyer was sprawled on the floor, and Talia, in a black sleeveless catsuit, her hair in a ponytail, was doing calisthenics in a corner.

"We did okay today," Sawyer said, nudging Cassidy's foot with his own. "Right? Looked like just about everyone on campus had a dirty car."

"And some had dirty cars more than *once*," Cassidy said, reaching up to pull her pack from beneath her head. Groaning with weariness, she sat up. "I had this guy in a black TransAm, who came back *three* times. And the really nutty thing was, the car was filthy each time. Even though I'd just scrubbed it from hood to trunk. Couldn't believe it! But," she waved the red pack in the air, "I'm not complaining, because we made fifty dollars off this guy!"

Sawyer whistled through his teeth. *"Fifty?* For three car washes! Didn't you give the guy change?"

"He wouldn't wait. The minute his car was clean, he tore out of the parking lot. Didn't you see him, Sawyer?" Cassidy unzipped her pack.

"TransAm? Don't remember. Look, it was a circus over there. After a while, all the cars blurred into one huge, multicolored mass of metal."

"The windows were tinted. Really dark." Cassidy pulled her cache of car wash funds from her pack, fingering through it for the three crisp new bills. "It's a really creepy feeling, looking into a car and seeing nothing. Like there might not be anyone in there." She moved her fingers through the thick pile of bills, expecting at any moment to encounter the bills that felt so different from all the others. But all of the bills felt soft and worn. They all felt used.

Where were those crisp, crackling *new* ones?

Although Cassidy went through the pile of bills three times, once rapidly and then twice again, more slowly, there were no crisp, crackling, brand-new bills.

There was no ten from the driver of the TransAm.

There were no twenties from the driver of the TransAm.

The money that had been thrust through the small window opening three different times by the driver in the cream-colored parka sitting behind the eerie, dark glass, was gone.

Chapter 3

When Cassidy had sorted through the pile of bills for the third time, she sank back on her heels, shaking her head. "It's gone," she said, glancing around the room with a perplexed expression on her face. "The fifty dollars is gone."

"You counted your money already?" Sawyer asked. "I haven't added mine up yet."

"No, I didn't count it. But the money I got from the guy in the TransAm was all brand-new. Three brand-new bills, one ten and two twenties. I could almost smell fresh ink on them." Cassidy glanced down at the pile of bills on the floor. "Not only are there *no* twenties in this pile now, there isn't a single new bill." She flicked at the pile with a finger. "These are all *old*."

Sawyer laughed. "Cassidy, that money might not be new, but it's still good."

"I *know* it's good, Sawyer," she cried, exasperated, "but you're *not* getting the point! There were three brand-new bills in my fanny pack when I left the parking lot. Fifty *dollars* worth! And now they're *gone*."

"Why would someone give you a twenty for a five-dollar car wash, and then not wait for his change?" Sophie asked. "Twice! That adds up to a lot of money, if you ask me."

Cassidy nodded. "I know. But the weirdest part was, I scrubbed that car spotless . . . and fifteen minutes later, there it was, back again, and *dirty* again."

"Must have been three different cars," Sawyer suggested matter-of-factly. "They just looked alike, that's all."

Cassidy explained about the tinted window glass and the dangling hearts on the door. "It was the same car each time," she said flatly. "That much I'm sure of. Anyone know who has a car like that?"

No one did.

"But you *did* see me washing it, right?" she persisted. "At least one of those times, you must have noticed it."

No one had.

"I didn't get there until the car wash was almost over," Talia reminded Cassidy. "And Ann said she and Sophie had just arrived, too."

"Sawyer, you were there," Cassidy said, a note of anxiety creeping into her voice. "You must have noticed it. It wasn't just an ordinary car."

But Sawyer shook his head. "I had my hands full. Wasn't really paying that much attention to other people's cars. Or maybe I'd taken a break."

"Never mind the car," Ann said. "What I want to know is, what happened to the money? If he really did give you fifty dollars, Cassidy, and you kept all the money you made in your fanny pack, it has to be there, right? Check the pile again."

Cassidy's head came up. Her eyes narrowed. "*If* he gave me the money? What's that supposed to mean, Ann?"

Ann ran a hand through still-damp, wavy hair. "Well, where *is* the fifty dollars?"

"Ann Ataska, what are you saying? You think that I made up the whole thing? Invented it? Imagined it?"

"Don't get upset, Cassidy," Sophie cautioned. "Ann didn't mean anything. But you sounded so positive that the bills were brand-new, and they're just not *there*, right?"

Sawyer added, "It was really wild down there, Cassidy. I had to stop a couple of times myself and check the bills I'd been handed."

"Oh, that's so patronizing," Cassidy cried. "You make it sound like I don't know my left hand from my right." She glanced at the faces in the room. And her heart sank as she realized what was happening.

No one in the room was convinced that she had ever had fifty dollars in brand-new bills in her possession.

Maybe they weren't even sure that the TransAm with tinted windows and red dangling hearts existed.

If this discussion continued much longer, *she* would no longer be sure of anything.

"Forget it," she said brusquely, jumping to her feet. She stooped to snatch up the bills and her pack. "Are we going to the movies or not?"

"Tell you the truth," Sawyer said, "I was kind of hoping we could take in a movie right here, downstairs." He glanced toward the wide window, sheeted with water. "It's pouring outside. I don't want to go back out in it for awhile. And it probably wouldn't be a good idea for you to get soaked again."

Cassidy's teeth clenched. "Right! I might get sick and start hallucinating that someone was stuffing brand-new twenty dollar bills into my hands. Which is pretty much what you all think happened this afternoon, right?" She couldn't believe it. Since when did Cassidy Kathleen Kirk imagine things?

There was an awkward silence.

To end it, Cassidy said lightly, "I'll just go brush my hair. Don't leave without me, okay?"

The sound of whispering outside the bathroom door as she brushed her hair made her furious. They were discussing her? Like a group of doctors consulting each other about a patient?

Well, there was *nothing* wrong with her!

She could remember the feel of those crisp bills in her hand, could hear the crackling when she slipped them into her pack.

She *couldn't* have imagined it.

But her hand shook slightly as she put down the hairbrush. It still shook as she handed the money over to be kept in the Quad safe downstairs on the way to the movie.

The movie hadn't started yet when they entered the basement rec center. A huge, square, wood-panelled room, it was packed with people. Except during midterms and finals, studying was not a popular Saturday night activity. Having fun, winding down after a week packed with classes, tests, papers and labs was the number one priority for most. On this Saturday night, the bad weather had limited off-campus activities, swelling attendance at the weekly movie.

As Cassidy and Sawyer took their seats, people began hurrying over to Cassidy to congratulate her on the success of the car wash.

"We must have hauled in a load of cash!" a girl named Tina said excitedly. The boy at her side, whose T-shirt read, "IF YOU CAN'T READ THIS, YOU'RE NOT CLOSE ENOUGH," added, "Leave it to Kirk here. If you want something to be a success, just get old Cassidy to run it!"

But Cassidy was having a hard time accepting their praise. True, the car wash *had* been a success. True, although the money hadn't been counted yet, she knew they *had* pulled in a load of cash! They'd be able to throw one great dance.

But they *should* have had fifty dollars more.

Had she lost the money? They'd been so busy. She might have thought she'd slipped the bills inside her pack, but with her eyes on the vanishing TransAm, maybe her fingers had missed the mark and the bills had fallen to the ground.

No. Not three times. And even once, she would have noticed. Or someone else would have.

Cassidy concentrated. Had she removed the

leather pack at any time after she'd been given the new bills?

Yes. Once during the car wash, to make change for a girl named Rita Nevins. And she hadn't put the pack back on right away, she remembered now. She'd dropped it onto the hood of a red pickup truck parked beside her, just long enough to brush her hair and sweep it up into a ponytail.

While she was bending over, brushing her hair, someone *could* have reached inside the pack and stolen a handful of bills.

Then, too, during the latter half of the day, the pack at her waist had become so wet, she'd slid it around so that it was at her back, in an effort to keep it drier. A really expert thief could have come up behind her . . .

A really expert *thief*? At a car wash? What was *wrong* with her?

Just before the lights dimmed, Cassidy saw Ann and her date arrive and make their way to a pair of seats up front. Ann's date was tall, with unruly dark hair. Travis. Ann Ataska's date was Travis McVey, who until very recently, had dated only Cassidy Kirk.

Talia, sitting on Cassidy's left, nudged her with an elbow, saying, "Well! When did *that* happen? How come she didn't tell us?"

"She *said* she had a date," Cassidy answered, sliding down in her seat.

"Yeah, but she didn't say it was Travis. Don't you think that's kind of weird?"

Then the lights dimmed, music began, and the screen lit up. Sawyer reached over and took Cassidy's hand. His hand felt warm and strong. Her own felt icy. She thought about Talia's question. Did she think that Ann's keeping silent about dating Travis was weird?

No. Ann probably hadn't been sure how Cassidy would react. Understandable.

What was *much* weirder was a black TransAm with darkened windows and dangling red hearts on the driver's door going through a car wash repeatedly. What was weirder was the disappearance from her fanny pack of three bills . . . the three crisp, brand-new ones given her by the unseen driver of the creepy car.

That's what Cassidy thought was weird.

Chapter 4

The dance to benefit the Twin Falls mental health clinic had been Cassidy's idea, with the full support of Dr. Bruin. Funds from the car wash would pay for dance expenses. Since the weather hadn't improved on Sunday, Cassidy invited everyone on the dance committee to suite 56A for a planning session.

"We made enough money from the car wash," she began when they were all seated or lounging on the floor, "to hold a really decent dance." She didn't mention the missing fifty dollars. "I think we should try to get Misstery to play. We can afford them." The group was a popular all-girl band on campus. Its lead singer, Lola Sturdevant, was a friend of Cassidy's.

Travis nodded. "That'll bring in a crowd. Are we selling tickets in advance or only at the door?"

I would be going to the dance with him, Cassidy couldn't help thinking, if we hadn't had that fight. Now Ann will probably be his date. I hope they have a wonderful time, she told herself. Not.

"I think we should do both," Ann suggested. "Sell them on campus, but sell them at the door, too." She directed a pointed glance at Sophie. "For those people who always wait until the last minute for everything."

Sophie always admitted freely that she was a procrastinator, and joked that she would do something about it — someday. Now she laughed ruefully. "Well, we all know *you* never forget anything, Ann."

"What about decorations?" Talia asked from her desk chair. "Any ideas?" Sheets of rain slapped against the window as they all mulled over the idea of a decorating scheme.

"Please," Talia added, "no red-and-white crepe paper streamers. I draped enough crepe paper in high school to last me a lifetime."

Cassidy nodded. "We need something more sophisticated. Black, maybe. Black and silver." Grabbing a sheet of paper and a pen, she began scribbling as she talked. "Black tablecloths, silver candleholders. Candlelight is so romantic." She flushed, remembering that both Sawyer and Travis were in the room. "I mean, the rec center isn't exactly the most glamorous place to have a dance. Candlelight should help."

"Black?" Sophie asked. She wrinkled her nose in distaste. "It's a dance, Cassidy, not a funeral."

"Black and *silver*," Cassidy insisted. "Maybe we'll put some red carnations on the tables if you absolutely must have color, Sophie."

"I absolutely must." Sophie looked satisfied.

But Sawyer complained, "Sounds expensive to me. We're cutting into our donation to the mental health clinic with every penny we spend. We didn't make *that* much on the car wash, did we?"

Cassidy flushed more deeply, wondering if Sawyer was deliberately reminding her of the missing fifty dollars. Deciding he wasn't, she answered, "We won't buy most of this stuff, Sawyer. We'll rent it. At that place in the mall. It won't cost that much. We'll go check it out this afternoon. They're open on Sunday."

But the supplies she ordered were more expensive than she'd anticipated. She, Sophie, and Talia took the small yellow shuttle bus to the mall after the meeting. They all had cars on campus, but the shuttle was free and ran often enough to be convenient.

Ann was baby-sitting again and couldn't go. When Cassidy complained, Ann said, "Look, the woman has her hands full with a job and three kids. And she pays well. She needs me more than you do."

That was true. It didn't take four people to order supplies.

The total for the rented supplies for the dance came to more than twenty dollars over the limit Cassidy had set.

"It's the silver," the clerk explained. "Silver always costs more, even rented. Perhaps you'd like to select a different color?"

But Cassidy had made up her mind. She could picture the setting: the tables covered in floor-length black tablecloths, adorned with silver candleholders and tall red candles, a single red carnation in a silver vase on each table.

If she only had that extra fifty dollars.

"No," she said firmly, "we'll stick with the black and silver."

The clerk took her student I.D. and telephone number and wrote up the order. Cassidy arranged to pick up the decorating supplies a few days before the dance.

They went to the food court for dinner. Pleased with having accomplished the ordering, Cassidy was contentedly munching on a carrot stick when Sophie suddenly elbowed her and whispered, "Heads up! Ex-boyfriend on your right!"

Cassidy turned her head. Travis was standing in line at the egg roll booth. And Ann was with him.

"She said she was *busy*," Sophie complained.

"She *is*," Cassidy said grimly, returning her attention to her carrot stick. She bit down so hard, she nearly chipped a tooth.

"The disintegration of a close relationship," Talia announced, "can produce the same symptoms as post-traumatic stress disorder." All of the psych majors tossed psychiatric terms around like slang, but Cassidy privately thought Talia was the worst. Maybe because she'd been hearing them all her life. "Sleeplessness or sleeping too much, loss of appetite, depression, nervousness, absentmindedness, an inability to concentrate, heavy-duty nightmares. It's all in chapter fifteen of our psych book." Her strong, smooth face solemn, she peered into Cassidy's face. "Haven't you read that far yet?"

"No. Maybe I'll skip that chapter." Cassidy plucked a ripe cherry tomato from her salad, but before popping it into her mouth, she added, "And I don't know why you're telling me this, Talia. I don't have any of those symptoms. I am not suffering from post-traumatic whatever. Not over a boy, I'm not!"

Sophie looked doubtful. "I don't know, Cassidy. You *did* lose that money from the car wash. Couldn't that be considered absent-mindedness?"

Cassidy lifted an eyebrow. "Sophie, you're not convinced that I ever *had* that money. But I *did*, and I didn't *lose* it." She pushed her salad bowl away and then, remembering that Talia had mentioned "loss of appetite" as a symptom of heartbreak, hastily retrieved it. "I think someone took that money."

"Well, I don't see how someone could steal something from your fanny pack, even if you took it off and put it somewhere," Sophie argued, "when the car wash was so crowded. Wouldn't a thief have been noticed by someone?"

"But that's just it," Cassidy persisted. "A thief could get away with something like that *because* it was so crowded. You know things get stolen on campus, Sophie. No one wants to admit it, but it's true."

"I guess. But," Sophie took a long swallow of soda, "why wouldn't a thief have grabbed *all* of the money from your fanny pack? Why just those three brand-new bills? That doesn't make any sense."

"No," Cassidy admitted, "it doesn't." Unfortunately, she had no explanation that did make sense. That confused her. She didn't like not understanding something. She wasn't used to it.

Talia and Sophie intended to continue shopping. "Talia has great taste," Sophie said. "She can help me pick out the perfect dress for the dance."

Cassidy decided to return to the dorm to finish her psych paper. She shot a resentful look in Travis's direction. Why hadn't he given her original paper to Bruin, the way he'd promised he would?

Travis and Ann stood up, ready to leave. They made a great-looking couple, Cassidy admitted reluctantly to herself. Travis so dark, Ann so fair. Still, it wasn't Ann's beauty that Cassidy envied. It was her manner. Quiet, tranquil, always appearing to be in total control. She was popular with the professors on campus as a baby-sitter because of her calm, organized manner. They liked the way Ann Ataska handled college life. And, Cassidy supposed, the way she handled children.

Telling Talia and Sophie good-bye, forcing herself not to glance again in Travis and Ann's direction, Cassidy left the food court.

She was halfway to the main entrance when she felt the familiar constriction in her chest. Oh, no, not now! She couldn't stand the thought of gasping and wheezing in the middle of the mall, with people all around. Sometimes, during a really bad attack, she doubled over in her struggle to breathe. People would stare at her and ask her if she needed help. She hated that.

I took my medication this morning, she thought angrily. Why is this happening now?

Darting into a hallway that led to a side exit, she turned her back to the mall and whipped out the inhaler she always carried in her purse. It was much more important than lip gloss or a comb.

She had caught the attack in time. The inhaler worked. On rare occasions, it didn't, usually because she'd ignored the symptoms too long, stubbornly refusing to admit what was happening. She no longer did that very often. The price she paid for stalling was too high. This time, however, she'd caught it early. But although her breathing had regulated itself, she felt a little weak, and headed for a rest room. She rested on the lounge there until her legs felt completely solid underneath her again. Then she stuffed the inhaler back in her purse and went back out into the mall.

She knew perfectly well why the medication hadn't done its job. Like it or not, the sight of Ann and Travis together at the food court had caused an emotional reaction. Stress. Not good for her.

Angry with herself for letting her emotions cause a physical reaction, Cassidy pushed the front glass door open with more force than necessary.

And came to a halt on the other side as she saw what was idling at the curb a few feet away.

A black TransAm.

There were no other cars sitting at the curb. Just that one. Waiting, its engine murmuring steadily.

Cassidy stood alone under the mall's marquee, a thin curtain of sleet flying around her. She could see the car clearly. It might not be the same one, of course, she told herself as she hesitantly moved forward. There had to be more than one black TransAm in the area of campus and the town of Twin Falls.

The passenger's side was facing her, so if there were red hearts fastened to the driver's door, they weren't visible from where she stood.

Cassidy wasn't sure what kept her from rushing to the driver's side to thank him for his generous contribution to the car wash. Maybe the fact that she no longer had the money? She wasn't willing to admit to him that she'd lost it. She'd feel like a fool. And telling him it was missing would sound as if she were hinting for more money.

Or maybe it was the fact that he'd been so reclusive, barely rolling his window down, not chatting with her like the other customers, not letting her see his face. If he valued his privacy that much, she probably shouldn't bother him.

But her curiosity had been aroused. She felt a sudden urge to know, at least, whether or not it was the same car. That seemed important, although she wasn't sure why.

The car's engine roared.

But it remained sitting at the curb.

Cassidy took a deep breath, let it out, and hurried over to the car, walking around behind it to the driver's side.

There they were, two strung-together plastic red hearts dangling like a small child's mittens, on the door handle.

The engine roared again.

If she was going to do anything, she decided, she'd better do it quickly before he took off.

Impulsively, she rapped on the dark glass of the driver's window.

Nothing happened.

She rapped again, more insistently this time.

Still no response.

Cassidy felt foolish, standing beside a car whose windows remained closed to her.

If he wasn't going to acknowledge her, she might as well leave.

Shrugging, she turned away from the car to walk around the front of it and back to the curb to wait for the shuttle bus.

But as she moved, so did the car.

It moved slowly, quietly, inching forward almost imperceptibly, keeping apace of Cassidy's steps, barring her way back to the curb.

She stopped, confused. What was he doing? She couldn't walk around in front of the car when it was moving. Was he leaving? Maybe he wanted to leave, but was afraid of hitting her.

She stepped back, away from the car.

It stopped moving, its engine still murmuring quietly.

Well, *one* of us has to move, Cassidy thought impatiently, and strode forward.

The car slid forward, too, maintaining an effective barrier between her and the curb.

What kind of game was he playing?

Whatever it was, she didn't like it. The sleet had increased, the tiny drops of ice stinging her cheeks, and she was cold. She hadn't worn boots, and her toes, in black flats, were freezing.

Okay, if she couldn't move around the front of the car to get to the curb, she'd go around the back way. What difference did it make?

As she turned, she heard the faint sound of another engine. When she looked up, she saw the yellow shuttle bus in the distance, aiming for the mall. Her ride back to campus. Her ride back to a nice, warm room and a robe and warm, dry socks on her icy toes.

All she had to do was get to the curb. There it was, a few feet away, on the other side of the black TransAm.

But . . . suddenly, she was afraid to move. What if he backed up just as she came around behind him? He'd hit her. Not hard, he wouldn't be going fast enough for that. But still, the car was heavy, and made of metal. She wasn't. Wouldn't it hurt?

I'm being ridiculous, she told herself. He's not going to run into me. Why would he? I haven't done anything to him.

Making up her mind, she strode to the back of the car and was about to dash around behind it when the TransAm moved. Quickly. The driver gunned the engine and the car raced backward, brushing against Cassidy's left shin as it did so, then screeching to a halt beside her.

Crying out in anger, Cassidy jumped out of the way. Shocked at how close a call it had been, she shouted, "That's not funny! Stop it now, just stop it! Get *out* of my way!" Furious, she reached out and slammed a fist down on the trunk of the car. "Let me go!"

The car stayed where it was. The murmuring engine seemed to be laughing at her.

Cassidy glanced around her in frustration. No shoppers emerged from the mall, no cars pulled into or out of the parking lot, and the yellow shuttle bus had stopped some distance away to load or dislodge passengers. There was no one around to see her plight. And there was no one around to help.

She was alone and at war with a huge hunk of black metal and its invisible driver.

Chapter 5

Cassidy stood beside the car, overwhelmed by helpless fury. Her knees began to shake, and she could feel the familiar tightening in her chest.

Don't panic, don't panic, she warned, clenching and unclenching her fists. Stay calm, you can't afford to have an attack now. Stay *calm!* This is silly. The curb is right there, just a few feet away. And he's *not* going to run over you. He's just tormenting you. Someone will come out of the mall and scare him off. The shuttle bus is on its way. Relax, just relax.

But relaxing was impossible. She was cold and frightened and frustrated and furious. Why was he doing this? What possible reason could the eerie, invisible driver have for tormenting her?

She would have to stop shaking, pull herself together, and make an end run for the curb.

Catch him off guard, race around the car when he was least expecting it.

So she forced herself to stand quietly, stilling her trembling limbs, for long, agonizing minutes. Didn't move a muscle. Her ears strained for some sound of the approaching shuttle bus. The driver of the TransAm would see the bus in his rearview mirror, and he'd leave. He couldn't keep up his torturous game with witnesses on the way.

But she heard nothing. What was taking the bus so long? When she felt that she couldn't stand still another second without screaming, she turned her head to the right to see where the shuttle was. Her heart sank. The small yellow vehicle was still much too far away, and stationary. The driver was standing outside the bus, scraping at the windshield. Great. Couldn't that have waited until he got to the mall?

Cassidy's temper snapped. Enough! This was ridiculous. She had no idea why she was being held prisoner by the black TransAm, but it was going to end *now*. It was time for an end run. She would catch the driver by surprise and make it to the curb before he noticed that she'd moved.

She tried.

Taking another deep breath, she dashed forward, behind the car.

She almost made it. She was only inches from the safety of the curb when the TransAm suddenly careened backward with a roar. Its rear bumper slammed into her left ankle and foot, sending a shaft of pain up her leg.

The blow surprised and stunned her, but she didn't stop. Instead, in one final, desperate lunge, she flung herself onto the curb, landing hard and pulling her legs in after her. She cried out as the palms of her hands and the right side of her face scraped against the cement.

With a triumphant honk of its horn, the TransAm jerked to a halt, gunned its engine, and then raced away with a screech of tires.

Cassidy roused herself enough to stare after the car, straining to read the license plate as the TransAm disappeared. But the plate was covered with mud. Deliberately? she wondered.

She lay there for a few minutes more, aware that a cold dampness was seeping through her slacks. And still the shuttle failed to arrive and dislodge riders to rush to her aid. Nor did the doors to the mall open and send forth shoppers to help her up from the curb. Cassidy felt as if the planet had been deserted, leaving only herself . . . and the black TransAm.

Afraid that the car would return, she pulled herself upright, conscious of a painful throbbing sensation in her left leg. Checking, she found a tear in her jeans that ran from her knee to her ankle. The exposed skin was torn and bleeding.

"It's just a scratch," she murmured, pulling the torn fabric together in a futile effort to cover the abrasion. Her tan raincoat was long, and would cover most of the rip.

She stood up, glancing over her shoulder to locate the shuttle bus. Still parked. But the driver was no longer standing outside. "It'll be here in a minute," she told herself in a shaky voice. "It'll be here, and I'll climb on and ride back to campus. I'll take a nice, hot shower, put on my robe and a pair of warm, dry socks and crawl into bed and forget this ever happened."

She knew that last part was a lie.

It felt like hours before the bus finally pulled up in front of her. Darkness was falling, and the temperature fell with it. Cassidy was shaking now not from fear, but from sheer cold. She had never been as glad to see anything as she was the squat, yellow bus when it finally skidded to a stop in front of her.

"Hey, wait for us!" she heard from behind her as she awkwardly made her way up the steps, one hand holding the raincoat firmly over the rip in her jeans. Turning, she saw Talia and Sophie running from the mall. "Hold the bus, Cassidy!"

Since the driver had already seen them, Cassidy moved down the aisle to take a seat at the back.

Talia and Sophie, packages in hand, their hair and jackets wet with sleet, joined her there a minute or two later.

"You must have been waiting for the bus *forever*, Cassidy. Look, I got a dress!" Sophie cried triumphantly. "You should see it, it's beautiful . . . what happened to your leg, Cassidy? It's bleeding!"

Cassidy had hoped the raincoat would keep them from noticing. But it wasn't quite long enough. "I slipped and fell," she fibbed. She was *not* going to tell them about the car. They hadn't believed her about the car wash, and that wasn't nearly as bizarre as what had just happened. They'd never believe that she'd been held "prisoner" by the very same car. "It's slippery out there."

Sophie nodded. "I almost fell, too. That cut looks pretty nasty. You've got a scrape on your cheek, too. Want to stop at the infirmary?"

"Don't need to. It's nothing. I'll clean it up myself. What'd you buy?" She didn't want to talk about her leg anymore. Didn't want to think about it, either. That might not be so easy. She could picture the car, see the dark window glass hiding the driver, feel the blow to her legs as the TransAm raced backwards . . .

She didn't hear a word Talia and Sophie said about their shopping.

Suite 56A at the Quad had never seemed so welcoming, a hot shower so comforting, her white terrycloth robe so luxurious, a pair of thick white socks so soft. The scrape on her leg, once it had been washed and disinfected, was less serious than it had looked. But it hurt, and her ankle had discolored and was beginning to swell. She could only hope it wasn't worse by morning. She didn't want to miss any more classes.

Although she felt totally drained and yearned to nestle into her bed, she took a few minutes to quickly type out a letter to Mistery, asking them to play at the dance. When she had signed and addressed the letter and sealed the envelope, she put it on a small stack of other envelopes waiting to be mailed. Someone would take them to the campus post office early the next morning.

That done, she crawled into bed. I'm lucky my leg wasn't broken, she thought as she snuggled under her comforter. Why would someone want to break my leg? Scare me half to death? Why would someone *do* that?

She had no idea.

It wasn't until, feeling completely warm and safe, she was slipping over the edge of consciousness into a deep, dreamless sleep that she remembered the psych paper. She hadn't done it. Bruin would be expecting it, and it wouldn't be forthcoming.

Unwilling to drag herself out of a warm bed to struggle through the assignment, Cassidy burrowed deeper into the covers, telling herself it wasn't her fault, anyway. It was Travis's. She'd finished the paper when she was supposed to. It wasn't her fault he'd lost it. If he really had.

She'd just have to tell Bruin she hadn't finished it yet. After what had just happened to her, the paper didn't seem all that important.

Willing herself to ignore the painful throbbing in her left leg, Cassidy gave herself over to the luxury of sleep.

She awoke the following morning to a quiet, empty suite. The others had gone off to breakfast without her?

At first, Cassidy was hurt by the realization. They always ate breakfast together on Mondays, Wednesdays, and Fridays because they shared the nine o'clock psych class. Why hadn't they waited for her?

Talia and Sophie had seen her leg when it looked its worst last night. They'd probably decided that she wouldn't be going to classes today, and had told Ann about the injury.

But I told them I was fine, Cassidy thought, annoyed. She glanced at her alarm clock. It was only eight o'clock. She had time to dress and even eat, if she wanted to, before class. She could catch up with the others if she hurried.

Hurrying, she quickly discovered, was out of the question. Her leg was too stiff and sore. And she had wasted ten precious minutes hunting for her wristwatch, which she always left on her nightstand. It wasn't there. And it wasn't in the bathroom, where she thought she might have left it when she was cleaning the wound on her leg.

She finally gave up, aware of passing minutes. She'd have to look for it later. By the time she left the room, dressed in warm wool slacks and a heavy sweater, the clock on her nightstand read eight-fifty. She was cutting it pretty close. Class started at nine, and Bruin hated tardiness. Arriving late wouldn't help when she had to explain that she didn't have the assignment.

Since her roommates hadn't returned, Cassidy guessed they had taken their books with them to breakfast. Sometimes they did, to save time. She'd be walking to class alone this morning.

She tried again to hurry. But it was hopeless with her leg so stiff and swollen. She hated walking into a classroom after everyone else was seated, but it was going to happen this morning. What a way to start a new week!

As it turned out, she didn't have to walk into the classroom at all. Because when she arrived at the psych 101 room, the door was open and everyone was coming out.

"Has class been cancelled?" Cassidy asked the first person she saw, who happened to be Travis McVey. Classes were occasionally cancelled for various reasons: a professor's illness, unusually bad weather, an important seminar that required a teacher's attendance.

"Cancelled?" Travis frowned down at her. "No. It's over. Where were you?"

"Over? It can't be over." Cassidy glanced down at her wrist, and realized she wasn't wearing her watch. "It's only nine o'clock."

"It's *ten* o'clock," Ann said, arriving at Travis's side. Sawyer, flanked by Talia and Sophie, was right behind her. "You're an hour late."

"That's crazy," Cassidy said, feeling heat rise in her cheeks. "I checked my clock. It said eight o'clock when I woke up. Not nine. Eight."

Ann shook her head. "*We* got up at eight. Sophie said you hurt your leg last night and probably wouldn't be going to class, so we decided to let you sleep."

"It was *eight* o'clock," Cassidy insisted stubbornly. "I *know* how to tell time."

Sawyer shrugged. "Don't get all bent out of shape. So you missed Bruin's class. It was boring, anyway. Talia and Ann Freud here were the only two paying attention. Sophie was daydreaming about the dance and everyone else was dozing. So forget it."

Cassidy couldn't forget it. Easy for them to dismiss it. *They* hadn't missed a class they couldn't afford to miss. "I know what I saw," she persisted. "My clock said eight o'clock."

"And your watch?" Travis asked. "Did your watch say eight o'clock, too?"

Her flush deepened. "I couldn't find my watch. I had it last night, but it wasn't on my nightstand this morning. I don't know where it is." Glancing around the group, studying their faces, she saw the same doubt in their expressions that she'd seen when she told them about the missing money from the car wash.

And she felt every bit as alone as she had the night before, when she was lying, stunned, on the curb outside the mall.

"That clock read eight o'clock," she said, biting off her words. Then she brushed past them and went into the psych room to face Dr. Bruin.

When she came back out, two red spots of embarrassment high on her cheekbones, the hallway was empty. She had hoped Sawyer would be waiting for her, but he wasn't.

She walked back to the Quad alone, anxious to reassure herself that she had not read the clock wrong.

Sawyer was waiting for her outside the dorm. So. He hadn't abandoned her, after all.

Noticing her limp, he asked with concern, "What happened to your leg?"

"I fell." She wasn't about to tell the bizarre truth to someone who was already questioning her ability to read a clock correctly. Maybe she'd tell him later, but not now.

Sophie, Talia, Ann, and Travis were already back in the room when Cassidy and Sawyer entered. It seemed to Cassidy that the three exchanged a look of concern when they saw her.

That annoyed her, and she hurried over to her bedside table, anxious to prove herself right. She reached down and picked up her alarm clock. "There!" she said triumphantly, holding it up and turning it toward them so they could all see its face. "What time does that say?"

There was a long moment of silence. Then Sawyer said quietly, "It says ten-fifteen, Cassidy. Not nine-fifteen. Ten-fifteen."

Sophie nodded, her eyes huge.

"What?" Cassidy whipped the clock around to face her. Sawyer was right. The clock now showed the correct time.

After another long moment, Cassidy slowly, silently, bent to replace the traitorous clock on her nightstand.

And saw her watch.

It was lying exactly where it was supposed to be. It was lying in the same spot where she placed it each night after she climbed into bed. Exactly where it *hadn't* been earlier that morning when she'd spent ten minutes searching for it.

Chapter 6

Cassidy stared at the watch. The silence in the room was as thick as pudding.

"Maybe there was something lying on top of your watch when you got up this morning," Sophie said helpfully. "So you couldn't see it."

Cassidy lifted her head. "There wasn't," she said shakily. "I'd have noticed if there had been. The watch just wasn't there."

When no one said anything, she added fiercely, "It *wasn't* there."

Still no one said a word.

I don't like this, Cassidy thought nervously. Something is *really* wrong. "Could someone have been in our room?" she asked.

"Someone?" Ann echoed in astonishment. "Like who?"

"I don't know." Cassidy knew she was clutching at straws. Why would someone come into their room simply to tamper with her clock and hide her watch? That was too ridiculous. But she was desperate for an answer. "All I know is, my watch wasn't on this table when I left this morning."

"Well, it's here now," Sawyer interrupted heartily, clearly anxious to have the unsettling business behind them. "All's well that ends well. Want to go downstairs and get something to eat?"

Everyone looked at Cassidy. She could see that they all hoped she would answer yes. Then they could go to breakfast and forget all this craziness. That's what they were hoping would happen.

And why not? What was the point of continuing to stand here and insist that her watch had been missing when no one believed her? Did she still believe it herself?

She wasn't sure. She *had* been sure, but now . . .

What, she wondered, did her friends think *had* happened? Did they think she had forgotten how to read a clock correctly? That she couldn't find her own watch when it was staring her right in the face? They were already convinced that she didn't know the difference between a brand-new, crisp bill and an old, smooth, used one.

"Do you think I was seeing things?" she

couldn't resist asking. "Or, in the case of my watch, *not* seeing them?"

"No one said that, Cassidy," Ann said calmly. "It's just that you've been sick, and then you took that bad fall yesterday. That must have shaken you up some. Besides, anyone can look at a clock wrong. I've done it lots of times."

"No, you haven't," Cassidy said, her voice cool. "Not you, Ann." But it was hopeless, she could see that. She was never going to convince them that the clock had been an hour slow, or that her watch had been missing.

She was glad now that she hadn't tried to tell them about the TransAm tormenting her yesterday at the mall. The looks of doubt on their faces now would be nothing compared to their reactions to such a crazy story. She'd been right to keep it to herself.

She suddenly felt very tired, as if she'd run a long distance. Maybe they were right. It *had* been a rotten week. She hadn't been herself. Maybe she still wasn't. It was easy to oversleep when you were exhausted. Then you woke up, looked at the clock, and saw what you wanted to see, right?

Sophie was probably right: The watch must have been on the table the whole time. Maybe it had slid underneath the clock. Yes, that could explain it. It had been hiding underneath the clock and when she picked up the clock just now to show them, presto, there was the missing watch.

"You're right," she said quietly, "I know you're right. I was tired, and . . ."

"You need something to eat," Sawyer said quickly. "Didn't eat breakfast, I'll bet. Did you?"

"No. I'll do that now."

As they all left, she couldn't help glancing over her shoulder toward her nightstand, where the clock sat staring out into the room, its hands smugly pointing out the correct time.

She had been so sure the small hand had been on the eight when she awoke that morning. Not on the nine. On the eight.

Being so wrong about something so simple, so basic, left her feeling like she had a big hole in her stomach.

But maybe that was just hunger.

Her leg ached all the way through a day of classes, a dance committee meeting, and a visit to the library to work on her psych paper, with a side trip to the post office to pick up mail. While she was there, she picked up the mail for her suitemates too: A care package from Sophie's grandmother, who made the best chocolate chip cookies in the world, a letter for

Talia, the return address the hospital where her mother worked, two postcards for Ann from friends in other schools, circulars from the campus bookstore, and four small, purple envelopes decorated with Salem University stickers.

She was walking back from the PO to the Quad, alone, when she spotted the black TransAm. It was parked in front of the Quad, its engine idling.

Cassidy stopped walking. She was by the fountain in the commons, a large, rectangular patch of green located near the Quad. The sight of the car made her knees weak, and she sank down on the stone wall around the fountain.

What was the car doing there? Waiting for *her*? Hadn't he tormented her enough yesterday? She didn't feel up to playing another nasty game of tag. But she couldn't get into the Quad without passing the car.

Of course you can, a little voice in her head said. The Quad is a huge complex. It has more than one door, silly. Pick door A, pick door B, pick any one of a dozen other entrances.

Cassidy shook her head and laughed softly to herself. Of course. What was the matter with her? She could simply retrace her steps to a side entrance and go in that way. She didn't need to go anywhere near that creepy car. And there were no driveways on the commons, so the car couldn't follow her.

Still a little shaky, but relieved, she got up and hurried to a side entrance, pulled the door open, and went inside. She never once looked over her shoulder toward the waiting car.

"Look," she said when she entered the suite and found Sophie coming out of the bathroom, her hair dripping wet, "invitations." She handed Sophie her mail.

Sophie glanced up with interest. "No kidding? A party, what fun!" she said, and ripped open the envelope. "Oh, great, it's at Nightingale Hall! I'm dying to see the inside of that place. Cath Devon's giving it. Ann's friend. And she's my partner in art class. I didn't think she was the party type. She's kind of shy and quiet. You never know about people, do you?"

Nightingale Hall was an off-campus dorm some distance up the road from Salem University. A huge, old brick house sitting at the top of a hill, surrounded by tall, dark oak trees, it had been the subject of rumors on campus. Someone had died there, although the details about the death were sketchy. *Nightmare Hall*, everyone called it now.

Cassidy thought a party sounded like fun, but she wasn't really interested in Nightmare Hall. Although she liked big old houses, she preferred them to have a cheerful look. Had Nightmare Hall belonged to her, she would have painted it a crisp white or a mellow yellow, repaired the tilting front porch, and painted the shutters and the front door a deep cranberry red, hung a bright red mailbox near the door. Anything to take away that creepy, old-horror-movie look the house had.

Still, a party might be nice. She barely knew Cath Devon, and was surprised to have been invited. Maybe her name had made its way onto the invitation list because she was Ann's roommate. Or because she was friendly with Jessica Vogt and Ian Banion, two residents of Nightmare Hall. They were in her math class. She liked both of them, and the party would be a good opportunity to get to know them better.

"I love Friday night parties," Sophie said. "We get to sleep late the next morning."

"Sophie, you love all parties," Cassidy teased. "You're a party animal."

"This is true," Sophie admitted. "That's because I never went to any parties in high school. Wasn't invited. Too fat for those unsophisticated high-schoolers." Pain flashed across her face.

"Well, you aren't fat. And you're invited to all the parties now."

"This, too, is true," Sophie agreed, and the pain disappeared from her eyes.

By the time Cassidy had taken a quick shower and applied fresh antiseptic cream to the abrasion on her leg, Ann and Talia had returned and opened their own invitations. "So," Cassidy said as she sat down on her bed and opened her own envelope, "is everybody going to this party?"

"I'm not sure," Talia said. "I'm running the next day. Probably shouldn't party the night before."

"Ms. Physically Fit," Sophie said. "If you can't be physically fit and still party, then I'll settle for poor muscle tone."

"I might have to baby-sit," Ann said. "Professor Benham is finally dating. Her husband's been dead over a year, so I say it's about time. She might be going out that night."

"There are other sitters, Ann," Cassidy pointed out. If Travis asked Ann to the party, would he be as annoyed with Ann for turning him down to baby-sit as he'd been with Cassidy for being busy with activities?

Ann shrugged. "I could use the money."

The talk turned to what to wear, and after a while, Cassidy rolled over and went to sleep.

She dreamed that she was being driven to the party at Nightmare Hall in the black

TransAm, but when they reached the long, curving gravel driveway up to the house, the car raced past it, and when she cried out a protest, the driver turned his head around to face her. But he *had* no face. No eyes, no mouth, no nose, no chin. There was only a cream-colored parka hood and a gray, foggy blank where his facial features should have been.

She awoke Wednesday morning shivering, her skin clammy and cold.

When she turned in the overdue psych paper, Professor Bruin said only, "About time."

The discussion in class that day centered again around the fragility of the human mind.

Cassidy, drowsy in the overheated room, rested her chin on her hand, her eyelids heavy. That nightmare had robbed her of a decent night's sleep. Who did that horrible car belong to? And why was it haunting her? She was so tired. She had never been so tired.

"Fatigue," the professor said as she strode back and forth, front and center in the large lecture hall, "can damage our immune system, weaken our resistance."

Tell me about it, Cassidy thought, listening now.

"And stress, too, has the ability to weaken our resources. Under certain circumstances, even the strongest ego can slip over the edge of sanity, given enough reason."

Someone in the group made an audible sound of disbelief.

"It's true," the professor continued, nodding her head for emphasis. "Many factors have the ability to weaken our hold on sanity. Illness, fatigue, depression, loneliness, shock, all of those things and more batter our senses, making us vulnerable to the ordinary stresses of everyday life. You're all fond of the expression 'losing it.' That is most likely to happen when we are overburdened with stress of one sort or another. No matter how strong we think we are, certain stimuli, such as the ones I mentioned above, can convince us that we're seeing things we really aren't, hearing sounds no one else hears, can take from us the ability to perform the simplest tasks. This is why managing your time and your physical and emotional resources well is so important."

Cassidy sat up straighter. "Seeing things?" "Losing it?" "Overburdened?" What was Professor Bruin *talking* about?

Involuntarily, Cassidy's head swivelled and she found herself looking straight into Travis's dark eyes. He was nodding knowingly, as if Professor Bruin had said aloud, "Cassidy Kirk, I'm talking about *you!*"

Maybe she is, Cassidy thought as she flushed and looked away, maybe she is.

Chapter 7

Cassidy was so busy Thursday and Friday, she hardly had time to catch her breath. There were two meetings of the dance committee, a science lab, two essays to write, dinner at Vinnie's (a popular pizza hangout), a movie with Sawyer Thursday night, errands to run. She had dry cleaning to take into town and one bicycle tire needed a slow leak fixed before the next Hike and Bike Club ride.

All of it seemed to take far more concentration than usual, and every time she walked across campus she found herself glancing around for any sign of the black car.

"Delegate," Sawyer suggested. "Quit trying to do everything yourself. You don't leap tall buildings in a single bound, do you? And I've never seen you changing into a blue caped outfit in a telephone booth. Delegate, Cassidy, it's the answer to a long life."

She decided he was right. She didn't need to do it all herself. So she asked Talia to take her sweaters to the dry cleaners when she took her own clothes in, and she asked Sophie if she would take Cassidy's bike to the campus shop to have the tire fixed.

She didn't ask Ann to do anything.

On Friday morning, Dr. Bruin asked her to stay after class.

Cassidy felt everyone's eyes on her. She groaned silently. What had she done now? She'd handed in the essay on the fragile human mind. Hadn't she done a good job?

"You have a test to make up," the professor reminded her when everyone else had left the room. "I gave it while you were sick. I'm a little surprised you haven't made arrangements to take it."

"I didn't know," Cassidy began, but she was interrupted.

"Be in my office at four this afternoon." With that, Professor Bruin picked up her leather attache case and left the room.

Four o'clock? Cassidy made a face. Darn! No one had said anything about a test being given while she was out sick. Well, at least she'd have time to take the test and still get back to the Quad early enough to get ready for the party at Nightmare Hall.

As she left the room, she hoped she was prepared for whatever questions Dr. Bruin might throw at her.

She didn't *feel* prepared. For much of anything.

Sawyer was waiting for her out in the hall. "Bad?" he asked sympathetically.

"No, I guess not. I have to make up a test. Why didn't you guys tell me she hit you with a pop quiz while I was out sick?"

"Forgot. Sorry. Listen, I can't see you tonight. Got some heavy-duty studying to do. Test in physics tomorrow morning, crack of dawn. How about tomorrow night? If we win the game with State tomorrow, there'll be a lot of celebrating. Wouldn't want to miss that, would we?"

He wasn't coming to the party at Nightmare Hall? Cassidy's disappointment was intense. It wouldn't be nearly as much fun without him. Unlike Travis McVey, who took life far too seriously, Sawyer knew how to have a good time.

But since Sawyer already seemed to feel bad, she didn't see any point in rubbing it in. As for partying two nights in a row, she'd earned it. She'd had worse weeks, but she couldn't remember exactly when or why. "Sure. What time?"

When they had made their plans, Sawyer

kissed her good-bye, and she headed straight for the library to cram for the psych test.

But when she got to Dr. Bruin's office that afternoon at four o'clock sharp, she received a second shock.

"Oh, heavens, I'm not giving you the test now!" the professor said as Cassidy unearthed a pencil from her backpack. "I have a faculty meeting. I only asked you here to set up a time for the test." She leafed through a thick, black notebook on her desk. "Seven o'clock tonight, here," she said briskly. "Be on time."

"Tonight? Seven o'clock tonight?"

"Would seven o'clock tomorrow morning be preferable?" the professor asked sharply, closing the notebook and standing up.

Seven A.M. the morning after the party? She'd have to get up at six. No way. "No, it's . . ." The test couldn't take that long. An hour? She could go back to the Quad now, shower and shampoo, dress in her party gear, come back and take the test and leave for the party from here. "It's okay. I'll be here."

"On *time*, please," Dr. Bruin repeated. "I have an engagement this evening."

Well, so do I, Cassidy thought resentfully as she left the office. There just weren't enough hours in the day, that was all. Maybe she should write to Congress about adding three or four more hours to each day. It was the only way she was ever going to get her life under control.

No one was in the suite when she arrived. A note in Ann's handwriting lay on Cassidy's bed.

Where were you? We waited, but Sophie was in a hurry to get to the mall. She forgot shoes last week, of course. What else is new? If she takes as long as she usually does, we'll have to catch up with you later. Ann.

Cassidy shrugged. Okay, she'd meet them at the party, just as she'd planned. It would have been more fun to leave the dorm together, but her grade in psych was already iffy. She couldn't afford to blow off this test.

She changed into brown velvet jeans and a cream-colored sweater, piled her hair on top of her head and fastened it with a tortoise-shell clip, pulling loose small pieces at the sides and back for a more casual look. Then she settled on her bed and munched on an apple while she studied her psych textbook, hoping the whole time that the door would burst open and her roommates would burst in.

They didn't.

She left the room at ten minutes before seven, remembering Dr. Bruin's warning about arriving at her office late.

The test took her ninety minutes. She had

studied all the wrong things, and had to struggle for half the answers. The class had only been given fifty minutes for the very same test. Still, while Cassidy appreciated being given the extra time, the hands on her wristwatch seemed to be ticking so loudly, she half-expected the professor to raise her head from the book she was reading and say, "Will you please be quiet?" Eight . . . eight-fifteen . . . eight-twenty . . . she wasn't going to arrive at Nightmare Hall much before nine.

Not that it mattered. Weekend parties were so informal, you could almost arrive any time. And it wasn't as if Sawyer was going to be there, waiting impatiently.

It wouldn't be as much fun without him. And if Travis was there, with Ann at his side, it would be even less fun. A lot less.

Cassidy nibbled on her pencil eraser. Maybe she wouldn't go. She *was* tired, and this test hadn't helped. Her head ached. If she hadn't already fixed her hair and changed her clothes, she'd be tempted to just go back to the room and sack out. Everyone else would be at the party, so she'd have complete peace and quiet. A great opportunity to get caught up on her rest. That way, she wouldn't be risking another asthma attack from fatigue and stress.

But she needed some fun. A little fun might

be better medication for her right now than sleep. And all of her friends, except Sawyer, would be there.

She would go. *If* she ever finished this killer test.

She finished. At eight-twenty-five, according to her watch.

"Have a good weekend," Dr. Bruin said as Cassidy handed her the completed sheets.

Easy for *you* to say, Cassidy thought. You didn't just blow your psych grade. Aloud, she said, "Thanks. You, too." Then she left the office.

She thought briefly about going back to the Quad, on the off-chance that her roommates hadn't left for the party yet. Maybe they'd waited for her. Glancing down at her watch again . . . eight-thirty . . . she knew it wasn't likely. Sophie liked to get to parties early.

Cassidy decided it would be faster to hop a shuttle bus for the short trip up the road. Taking her car would mean fighting for a parking space, and she was so late, the driveway at Nightmare Hall was probably already crammed full of cars.

When the bus pulled up in front of Nightingale Hall, there weren't as many cars as she'd expected parked in the gravel driveway that curved up the hill from the highway and around in front of the huge, old, dark brick house. Other people must have had the same idea she'd had . . . the shuttle bus. And a lot had probably walked, since the weather was halfway decent. Cold, but not raining or sleeting. And it wasn't about to, Cassidy decided as she trudged up the hill. She could see, through the bare-limbed branches of the gigantic oak trees sheltering Nightmare Hall, millions of tiny, silvery stars shining overhead. No rain tonight.

That seemed like a good omen. It would be nice if Sawyer could yank himself away from his studying to come to the party for a while, but even if he didn't, she was going to have a good time. She *needed* to have a good time.

As she climbed the wide, stone steps and stepped onto the wooden porch, she could hear laughing and talking inside. Sounded like a good time. Great.

She didn't bother ringing the doorbell. No one rang doorbells at parties. The door was kept unlocked, and you just walked in. That's the way it was done. Otherwise, someone would have to keep running to the door every few seconds until all the guests had arrived.

The front hall at Nightmare Hall was huge, with a high ceiling and a faded Oriental runner making its way across the hardwood floor. Cassidy had expected to see people gathered there, as they always were at a party, but the foyer was empty.

Music, she thought, surprised, where is the music?

The laughter and low-voiced chatter seemed to be coming from a room to her left. She followed the sounds until she stood in the open doorway of a large, square room. It wasn't an attractive room. The walls were painted a dark color, the window draperies and furniture old and faded. But there was a fire in the fireplace and the soft glow of lamplight gave the room a welcoming look.

There were a dozen or so people sitting on the old furniture or lounging on the carpet.

They looked up in surprise as Cassidy appeared in the doorway.

She took everything in very quickly.

There was no music.

There were no tables loaded with food and drinks.

The floor wasn't cleared for dancing.

There were no decorations of any kind, and the people in the room didn't look at all like they were partying. Not one of them had a cup or a plate of food in hand.

If there was a party at Nightmare Hall tonight, it hadn't started yet.

"Hi," Cassidy said, frowning slightly. "I'm

. . . I'm here for Cath Devon's party. Am I early? Did I get the time wrong? I thought the invitation said eight." Of course, she thought suddenly, feeling a little sick, I thought my *clock* said eight, too. But it didn't.

A tall, pretty girl with very short, dark hair stood up and came over to Cassidy. "Oh, Cassidy," Jess Vogt said with a gentle smile, "that party isn't tonight. It's not until *next* Friday night."

Chapter 8

Cassidy was painfully aware that everyone in the room already knew that she had recently shown up an hour late for a class. News like that traveled around campus faster than the common cold.

She drew herself up to her full five feet, two-and-a-half inches. "But I'm sure my invitation said the party was tonight," she protested. Even as she said it, she could hear again her own voice saying, "But I'm sure my clock said eight, not nine." Right.

But she *was* sure this time. Tonight's date had been on the invitation, printed neatly in black ink. She remembered thinking that it was pretty short notice for a party. She wouldn't have thought that if *next* Friday's date had been on the purple card.

"Maybe Cath made a mistake and put down the wrong date," Jess said in that same gentle voice. Her dark eyes were sympathetic.

She sounds like she's talking to someone who is feebleminded, Cassidy thought with a flash of resentment. She was immediately ashamed. Jess was just trying to be kind.

"I didn't make any mistakes," Cath Devon said, getting to her feet to join Jess and Cassidy in the wide doorway. "I don't make mistakes like that. You must have read it wrong, Cassidy."

As any feebleminded person would, Cassidy heard. She felt suddenly dizzy. "But there are all those cars out there," she said weakly, wishing the floor would open up and swallow her whole. By morning, everyone on campus would know that Cassidy Kirk had shown up for a party-that-wasn't.

"We're having a meeting," Jess explained. "Student government."

A meeting. The cars parked along the driveway were there for a meeting, not a party.

Cassidy took an awkward step backward, wanting desperately to escape. So many pairs of eyes looking straight at her, so many voices silenced by embarrassment . . . for *her*.

I should make a joke, she thought as she valiantly battled tears of humiliation. I should laugh and say something like, "Just wanted to check up on how our student government is doing, make sure you guys aren't goofing off."

But some inner instinct told her the joke would fall flat.

"I guess I must have read the invitation wrong, after all," she squeezed out between clenched teeth. "Sorry I interrupted your meeting." Then she turned and headed for the front door.

Cath followed. "You'll come next week, though, right?"

Cassidy almost laughed aloud. She's trusting me to get the time and date right? she thought bitterly.

"Sure!" she called over her shoulder as she yanked the front door open, hurried across the porch, and ran lightly down the steps, "I'll be here. Count on it!"

If she hadn't died of embarrassment by then.

She could feel Cath's concerned eyes following her down the driveway. The back of her neck felt like it was on fire. Although her legs moved like wooden boards, she walked as fast as she could, thinking that the driveway had lengthened by miles since she first went into the house.

Unwilling to wait for a shuttle, Cassidy began walking rapidly up the road toward campus. There was almost no traffic. *Normal* people who got their dates and times right were inside somewhere having a grand time and wouldn't be back on the road until it was time to go home. Only Cassidy Kirk, who seemed to be losing either her eyesight or her mind, was trudging along a cold, dark road all alone.

As she walked, huddled deep inside her leather jacket for protection against a sudden cold wind that swept out of the thick, black woods on her right, she remembered that Sawyer hadn't actually said, "I can't go to the party at Nightmare Hall tonight." He had said only, "I can't see you tonight." And then she hadn't mentioned the party because she didn't want to make him feel any worse than he already did about having to study.

And Ann's note, she remembered, hadn't said, "See you later at the party." Ann's words had been, "We'll catch up with you later." She hadn't said where.

But someone, sometime during the week, must have mentioned what night the party was taking place.

Yes, she remembered, they had. But each time, the actual date hadn't been mentioned, only the vague phrase, "Friday night." No one had said, *"next* Friday night." Just "Friday."

Because, she thought, scuffing her foot angrily, everyone took it for granted that any idiot who could read an invitation *knew* the party wasn't this week.

Cassidy had never walked up the road alone at night. She'd never had to. She decided she didn't like it. The wind from the woods made a harsh, eerie, whispering sound, tugging at her clothes and hair, stinging her cheeks. Campus suddenly seemed much further away than she'd anticipated when she began walking.

Headlights from a lone oncoming car illuminated the road briefly, then swept on past Cassidy. She was once again alone on a dark, deserted road.

She had been so absolutely certain about the date on that invitation.

What was *wrong* with her? This was so terrifying, seeing things that weren't there, getting things all wrong. Not like her at all.

She was so lost in misery that she never heard the car until it was right there beside her, a huge hunk of metal so black it was almost invisible in the darkness. As it slowly, quietly, pulled up beside her, the right sideview mirror gently nudged her left elbow.

Even before she turned her head to look, she knew it was the TransAm.

She stopped walking.

The car stopped, too, but its engine continued to murmur.

A scream welled up inside her throat, but she swallowed it. What good would that do? There was no one around to hear it.

What did he *want* with her? And how had he known she was out here?

Cassidy glanced uncertainly around her. The car was blocking access to the road. Not that it would do her any good to run in that direction, anyway. If there were cars, she'd run the risk of being splattered all over the blacktop, and if there weren't cars, dashing out onto the road wouldn't accomplish anything except making her a better target for the TransAm. And running into the woods would be stupid without a flashlight.

She was safer right where she was, on the berm of the road. If she had to, she could always dive into the ditch on her right, between the road and the woods. Half-filled with cold, muddy water from recent rains, it looked unappetizing. But the car couldn't follow her into the ditch.

One thing she was very sure of. She was *not* retreating to Nightmare Hall. The way they'd all looked at her when they realized she was there for a party . . . no way was she going to go running back there to say that an eerie, creepy car was stalking her.

The black lump of metal sat beside her, humming.

Murmuring.

Waiting.

It hadn't been a good day for Cassidy. First the surprise test, then the party mix-up, not a good day at all. I am *not* in the mood for any stupid auto-pedestrian games, Cassidy decided, and in a sudden burst of temper, kicked out viciously at the TransAm's right front tire. Her foot connected with a loud thunk.

She wasn't prepared for what happened next.

The car's horn bleated angrily in response to the blow. The engine roared, the wheels spun, spraying Cassidy with a shower of gravel before veering sharply to the right as if the car intended to drive straight across the water-filled ditch and into the woods. When the TransAm was positioned sideways on the berm, directly in front of Cassidy, the passenger's door suddenly swung open, slamming into her.

The suddenness of the maneuver caught Cassidy off guard. As the door flew open, she caught only a glimpse of the face hidden beneath a floppy, cream-colored hood before she was struck in her midsection. She let out a soft, startled cry of surprise as the blow knocked her off her feet. She flew backward, landing full force on her back in the grass beside the berm, the breath knocked out of her.

She was too stunned to move as the door slammed shut, the TransAm shot backward, spun around, and with a triumphant blast of its horn, roared away, up the road toward campus.

Chapter 9

Cassidy lay on her back next to the ditch, her right hand immersed in the icy water, as if she had decided to soak it. She pulled it free and sat up, shaking her head to clear it as she wiped the hand dry on her pant leg.

What had just happened?

She remembered kicking the car's tire and then . . .

Shuddering, she gingerly pulled herself to her feet, grateful that she hadn't landed in the muddy ditch. Had he meant to send her flying into that cold, filthy water?

Why? Why would he do that? What was he doing out here in the first place? Looking for *her*? Why? And how could he have known she would be out here?

Her legs felt very shaky. But she realized very quickly that she had a bigger problem. Her breathing wasn't stabilizing. Before she could stop it, the familiar cough rose up out of her chest and spilled out into the air, increasing in quantity and volume until her body was wracked with coughs. In minutes, the air filled with the harsh, wheezing sound of her tortured lungs. Ann, when she'd heard it, had called it in awe, "the agonized cries of a dying frog."

Doubled over, struggling for breath, Cassidy fumbled in her purse. She had one terrible, agonizing moment of dread when she remembered that she had switched purses for the party but couldn't remember whether or not she had switched her inhaler as well.

She had. An enormous sense of relief filled her as her fingers wound around the life-saving device. Gasping for breath, she yanked it from her purse, sending it directly to her mouth.

The epinephrine worked. She was still shaky from the blow to her midsection and the ensuing fall, but at least she was breathing again.

She wanted nothing more than to sink to the ground and sit on the grass for a while, until she felt one hundred percent again. But the TransAm was out there, somewhere, and could come back. Thoroughly frightened now of the black car and its unseen driver, she didn't dare wait by the side of the road.

As she began walking again, the inhaler still in her hand, she spotted the lights of Burgers

Etc., the long, silver diner across the road from campus. She could take refuge there. There would be people inside from school. Even if they weren't people she knew, she'd wait and walk across the highway with them. The car wouldn't attack her if she wasn't alone.

She couldn't run. Her chest still ached and she was sore all over from her encounter with the car. But she walked as fast as she could, and breathed a huge sigh of relief when she opened the door to the diner and hurried inside.

It was bright and cheerful, warm and welcoming, as always. But nearly deserted. Too early for a crowd. She slipped into a booth at the back, where she felt safe.

"You don't look so good," the waiter who brought her a glass of water said. "You okay?"

No, she wasn't okay. Not at all. She was so scared, her insides were quaking. The car could come back, looking for her. "I'm okay," she lied and ordered hot coffee.

She didn't recognize any of the half dozen students in the diner. But she felt warm and safe and the coffee was delicious. No reason why she couldn't just sit here and wait for someone she knew to come in. They would, eventually. It was Friday night. By that time, this ridiculous trembling might have stopped. And she might have stopped thinking that every car pulling into the parking lot was a black TransAm with tinted window glass.

Three more people came in before the door swung open and someone she knew entered the diner. Someone she knew very well. Or *had* known very well.

Travis Loyola McVey.

He came in alone. Cassidy watched and waited for a few seconds, expecting Ann Ataska to be right behind him. But she wasn't. Travis really was alone.

Her arm seemed to raise up into the air all by itself, as if it had a mind of its own. It was waving to Travis, signalling to him to join her.

When he saw the motion, which he clearly hadn't expected, he glanced over his shoulder to see if there was someone behind him she might be waving to. There wasn't. He hesitated, and then, shrugging, moved down the narrow aisle toward her booth.

They hadn't been alone since their argument. They had, of course, seen each other. It wasn't that big a campus, and Travis was in her psych class, on the dance committee, and in the Hike and Bike Club. But there had always been other people around.

He echoed the waiter's statement as he slid into the seat. "You look kind of weird. How come you're in here all alone? Where's Duncan?"

"Sawyer had to study." Cassidy hesitated, not knowing how much to tell him, if anything. If she told him about the car, which she really, desperately needed to tell someone, he'd ask her what she was doing walking alone on the highway, and then she'd have to tell him about the party-that-wasn't. Too mortifying. Anyway, if she was going to tell anyone, it really should be Sawyer.

It should be.

But Sawyer wasn't here. And Travis was.

"There's this car . . ." she began.

When she had finished, Travis shook his head. Several dark curls fell across his forehead, and Cassidy had to clench her fists to keep from reaching out and brushing them back into place. "You're not pulling my leg, are you?" he asked suspiciously.

She didn't blame him. "No. I'm telling you the truth. Do you know anyone who has a car like that?"

He shook his head again. "Nope. Campus is full of late-model sports cars, but I've never noticed a black TransAm. And I think I would have." He fell silent then, stirring his coffee absentmindedly, staring down at his cup.

Cassidy waited for him to say, "You know,

you've been under a lot of stress lately. Maybe you imagined the car. If you'd eased up on your extracurricular activities like I told you to, this wouldn't be happening."

But he didn't say any of that. Their conversation was awkward, both aware of underlying tension, but they talked about the upcoming dance, and the scheduled bike ride, and Travis didn't once suggest that Cassidy's imagination was overactive.

Ann did, though, when she, Sophie, and Talia arrived a few minutes later and squeezed in beside Travis and Cassidy. The look on Ann's face when she saw the two sitting together didn't escape Cassidy's notice. Ann's eyes narrowed and her mouth tightened, the way they did when someone in 56A borrowed one of her sweaters or blouses and tossed it on the floor after wearing it. "If you're through with it," she had said coolly more than once, picking up the garment and shaking out the wrinkles, "give it to me. I'll take better care of it than that."

She could easily, Cassidy thought as Ann slid in beside Travis, say the same thing to me about Travis.

Cassidy hadn't intended to tell the others about the car, but before she could stop Travis, he'd told them, ending the story by asking if any of them knew who might own such a car.

They all shook their heads no.

And Ann said casually, "Weird that no one saw it happen."

"There weren't any cars on the road just then," Cassidy said.

Ann nodded. "Um-hum. Cassidy, what on earth were you doing walking on the highway alone, anyway? Didn't you have a date with Sawyer tonight?"

The question Cassidy had been dreading had arrived.

She might as well tell them. They'd hear about her ill-timed arrival at Nightmare Hall soon enough. She'd rather they heard it from her first.

Forcing a light laugh, she said, "You're not going to believe this." But she knew they would. Unfortunately, they would.

They did.

Sophie and Talia were sympathetic, tossing off the mistake lightly, as if they did the same kind of thing every day. Which they didn't. Sophie was a procrastinator and Talia was a fitness nut, but they never got their days mixed up.

It was Ann's reaction that set Cassidy's teeth on edge. Ann put one hand on Travis's arm and said, her words laced with disbelief,

"I can't believe you read that invitation wrong. I mean, the lettering was so *clear*. I remember thinking how professional it looked. Cath is very artistic." Then she added with what sounded like genuine concern, "Cassidy, that medicine you take doesn't cause hallucinations, does it? I mean, there are lots of medications that do. Dr. Bruin has mentioned some of them in class. Maybe epinephrine is one of them."

Cassidy's cheeks grew warm. "You don't believe me about the car?"

"I believe that you saw a car. But no one in this booth has ever seen a car like that on campus, have we, guys?"

Sophie shook her head sadly, and Talia said, "I haven't. But that doesn't mean there isn't one."

"Thanks, Talia," Cassidy said, sliding out of the booth, her movements stiff. "Now, if you guys don't mind, I think I'll just take my addlepated brain and trot on back to campus before I start seeing little green men marching toward this booth carrying tiny little trays. I see Torey Mullins up there. I'll walk back with her."

She had already started down the aisle when Travis called, "Wait! I'll go with you."

"Then we all will," Ann said hastily, following Travis out of the booth.

"But I didn't get to eat anything!' Sophie complained. "I'm staying here. Talia, you'll stay, right?"

Talia stayed.

When Travis and Ann caught up with Cassidy, Ann said, "I'm sorry if I hurt your feelings, Cassidy. I didn't mean to. You're not mad, are you?"

Cassidy shook her head. How could she be mad? She hadn't really expected anyone to believe her bizarre story about the car. It had amazed her that Travis had listened. And she wasn't about to assume that he believed her, just because he'd listened. "No, Ann, it's okay."

But it wasn't okay. The walk back to school was awkward, with Travis walking between the two of them, Ann monopolizing the conversation by prattling on and on about the upcoming dance, and Cassidy continually glancing around her for some sign of the black car.

When they arrived at the Quad, there was another awkward moment when Cassidy held the door open for Ann, only to realize that Ann wasn't ready to come in just yet. She was hanging back, standing close to Travis on the walkway.

She wants me to go in so she can kiss him good night, Cassidy thought, and I'm standing here like an idiot holding the stupid door open. "See you," she said quickly, and spun around, closing the door behind her and hurrying to her room.

The first thing she did was stride to her desk and yank the drawer open, rummaging around inside until her fingers closed around the purple envelope. She pulled it out. Anxiety made her chest rise and fall rapidly as she slid the invitation from its casing. The date in black ink *had* to be today's date. It had to.

But it wasn't.

The date on the invitation was clearly next Friday's.

Nothing about the lettering suggested that it had been tampered with. The numbers weren't smudged or smeared.

Moaning softly, Cassidy sank down on the bed, the invitation still in her hand. She had been hoping, right up until the very last second, that it was Cath Devon who had made the mistake, not Cassidy Kirk.

But there it was, right in front of her. The mistake had been hers, and hers alone.

What is *wrong* with me? she wondered miserably. I can't even read a simple *date* without screwing it up in my head.

She felt foolish and embarrassed. But there was something else, too, something worse.

She was frightened.

What was happening to her mind? She was making some very major mistakes these days. That had never happened before. It wasn't like her. Not like her at all.

There couldn't be anything wrong with her medication. She'd been taking it for a long time now, and nothing like this had ever happened before.

Then what *was* it?

Absentmindedly, she checked her mail. A dental bill, an ad from the bookstore, and a long, white envelope addressed to her. No return address.

She slit the flap open with a fingernail and unfolded the letter inside. It was a typewritten acceptance from the musical group, Misstery. They would, it said, love to play at the dance being held by the psych majors. Not only that, Lola, who had signed the letter, added that because it was a fund-raising event, Misstery would waive its usual fee.

The letter greatly improved Cassidy's mood. They'd be saving a lot of money, thanks to Lola's generosity. Losing the fifty dollars from the TransAm wouldn't matter so much now.

She tried to call Lola to thank her, but there was no answer. Well, of course not. Lola wouldn't be home on a Friday night, she'd be out somewhere, performing. The phone call would have to wait.

It seemed like an awfully long time before Ann joined her in the suite, her cheeks rosy from being outside in the night air. The first thing she said was, "So, did you check out your invitation to the party? Did Cath really make a mistake?"

No point in lying. "No, she didn't. I guess I read it wrong."

No comment from Ann. She sat down on her bed and pulled a comb from her purse.

Cassidy didn't want to hear what Ann had to say, and when the phone rang, she grabbed up the receiver as if it were a life preserver.

It was Sawyer, wanting to know what she'd done all evening.

The whole time she was reluctantly telling him, reliving her humiliation at Nightmare Hall but leaving out the part about the TransAm, Ann sat on her own bed, winding her long, blond hair in pincurls and watching Cassidy as if she were solemnly regarding a species from another planet.

Cassidy turned her back to Ann, facing the wall instead.

When she finally relented and told Sawyer about the TransAm, because she didn't want him to hear it from anyone else, the doubt in his voice was so thick, Cassidy found it surprising that it was able to make its way through that skinny little telephone cord. Disappointed, she told him she had a headache, and hung up.

"If I were you," Ann said around the bobby pin between her teeth, "I'd have that medication checked out."

"And if I were you," Cassidy replied lightly, "I'd mind my own business." In the indignant silence that followed, she turned off her bedside lamp, pulled the comforter up around her shoulders, and flipped over on her side, her back to Ann again.

But it was a long time before she fell asleep.

Sawyer called early the next morning, when Cassidy was just coming out of the shower.

"It's for you," Ann said crisply, handing Cassidy the phone. "It's Sawyer."

Cassidy smiled, said "Thanks, Ann," and took the phone.

All three of her roommates left to get coffee.

Sawyer said, "I had Tom Lucas, a friend of mine who works in the administration building, run all of the car registrations on campus through the computer."

Cassidy gripped the receiver. She was about to find out exactly who on campus was using his very expensive, very impressive, but very creepy car as a weapon against her. Maybe when she knew who it was, she could figure out the *why* of it. And stop it from ever happening again. "Who?" she asked. "Who does the TransAm belong to? Is it someone I know? What's his name?"

"Cassidy," Sawyer began. He stopped, cleared his throat, and tried again. "Cassidy, there is no TransAm, black or any other color, registered at Salem University."

Chapter 10

"Tom checked twice," Sawyer said when Cassidy didn't respond. "He said Salem has more foreign sports cars than Beverly Hills, but no TransAm. Sorry."

When Cassidy found her voice, she said. "But I *saw* it! It's black, with tinted window glass."

"I didn't say you didn't see it." Sawyer's voice was sympathetic. "All I'm saying is, it didn't come from campus. It could be from Twin Falls, Cassidy."

"I don't know anyone in Twin Falls."

Her roommates entered the room. Sophie was carrying a cardboard tray filled with steaming Styrofoam cups. Cassidy took one gratefully and sipped from it. The hot coffee cleared her head. "I don't know a soul in town," she repeated as the trio went into Talia and Sophie's room.

"That doesn't mean anything," Sawyer pointed out. "The guy could be a psycho. He may have picked you at random, the way serial killers pick their victims."

"Whoa!" Cassidy cried, her eyes wide with alarm. "How did we get from weird car games to serial killers? And I'm *not* a victim, Sawyer."

"Not yet." Then he quickly added, "Look, I'm not trying to scare you. I just meant, someone who's really whacko, like we've talked about in psych class, doesn't need a reason to do things. Doesn't even need to *know* the people he picks on. So the car could belong to someone in Twin Falls, that's all I'm saying."

The idea that a stranger, someone she had never met, had targeted her, was far more frightening to Cassidy. If it were someone she knew, maybe someone she had inadvertently offended, she could approach the person, make amends, straighten things out. But a stranger, with no real motive, how could she deal with that?

She thanked Sawyer for his help, told him she'd see him at the football game that afternoon, and hung up. When she had taken her medication, washing it down with coffee, she went into Sophie and Talia's room. It was crowded with stuffed animals of Sophie's in all shapes and sizes, and Sophie was sharing her chair with a life-size stuffed alligator wearing jeans and a Salem sweatshirt. Ann was sitting on the foot of Talia's bed, filing her nails.

Cassidy decided against sharing Sawyer's news with them. None of them had ever seen the TransAm. If she told them that no such car was registered on campus, they'd think . . . well, she knew what they'd think.

"I called Cath and told her she didn't make a mistake on the invitation," Ann said. "I didn't think you'd mind. The remote possibility that she might have screwed up was driving her bananas."

Cassidy stiffened. Why did Ann have to bring that up? She didn't want to think about it this morning. "Cath didn't sound at all unsure last night," she said, sitting down on Sophie's bed. "She sounded absolutely positive that she'd put the correct date on every invitation."

"Oh, Cath might have sounded like that," Ann argued mildly, "but trust me, she was biting her nails. I told her the truth so she could relax."

Sophie's and Talia's silence made it clear to Cassidy that they, too, knew the correct date had been on her invitation. Ann must have been quick to set the record straight. She'd probably called Travis and told him, too. Cassidy could almost hear Travis's reaction: "Well, I *told* her she was going to self-destruct if she didn't slow down. I guess I was right."

"Thanks for sharing, Ann," she said, sarcastically.

"Cassidy," Talia offered, "if you want me to, I could talk to my mother. She might have some advice for you. And it wouldn't cost anything."

"Advice about what, Talia?" As if she didn't know.

Talia flushed. "Well, I just meant . . ."

"I know what you meant," Cassidy interrupted. "You think I need a shrink. All of you are thinking the same thing. Well, it seems to me that what I really need is an *eye* doctor. Anyone have one of those for a parent?"

Silence.

Turning to Sophie, Cassidy asked stiffly, "Sophie, have you had time to get to the bike shop? I've got that ride coming up."

Sophie flushed guiltily. "Oh, gosh, Cassidy, I'm sorry. I forgot! I'll do it this week, I promise. Your bike will be ready in time for your ride."

"Aren't you coming, too? You're a member. I thought that was why you were getting your bike chain fixed."

Sophie's flush deepened. "Can't. I forgot all about the ride and made a date with this really cute guy in my government class. But I'll still get the bikes fixed."

"Thanks, Sophie," Cassidy said, wondering at the same time if she shouldn't take her bike to the shop herself, just to be on the safe side.

But Sawyer had said, "delegate," and that's what she was doing. She couldn't throw her hands in the air the minute someone forgot something.

Anyway, look who's talking, she thought as she left the room. Sophie may put things off, but when's the last time *she* showed up at the wrong place at the wrong time. Or was it the right place at the wrong time? Whatever.

Getting the date wrong for the party had dealt Cassidy's self-confidence a serious blow. Before she left for the game, she found herself double-checking everything. Was her watch on her wrist? Had she switched her inhaler from last night's small clutch bag to her everyday shoulder bag? It was sunny out — were her sunglasses in her jeans pocket?

Remembering the severity of her asthma attack on the highway, she checked her purse three times for her inhaler.

"Come on, Cassidy," Talia said impatiently from the doorway. "We're going to miss kick-off."

"Sorry, I'm coming." Cassidy grabbed a blue

knit hat that matched her sweater, slung her purse over her shoulder, and hurried to the door.

"Too bad Ann had to baby-sit," Talia commented as they emerged from the dorm into a crisp, sunshine-filled day. Large and small clusters of students were headed across campus toward the stadium.

"She didn't *have* to," Cassidy pointed out. She was still annoyed with Ann for hinting that Cassidy was seeing things. And at Talia, too, for suggesting psychiatric help. "She could have said no."

"She's worried about her grade in that class. And I think she feels sorry for Dr. Benham, raising three kids by herself. Those kids are monsters. They drive Ann nuts."

"Well, at least she has an excuse," Cassidy muttered under her breath. No one heard her.

Cassidy wondered, since Ann was busy, if Travis would come to the game alone.

She was acutely conscious of eyes on her as they climbed up into the bleachers. Flushing painfully, she told herself she shouldn't be surprised. You *knew*, she scolded silently, that everyone on campus would hear about the invitation screwup. They're staring at you because they're curious about what kind of an idiot goes to a party on the wrong night. Can you blame them?

She tried to shrug off the stares, but when they were seated, halfway up in the stands at the forty-yard line, she could hear whispering behind and around her.

It disgusted her. Why were they making such a big deal out of a silly little mistake?

And then she realized that it couldn't just be that. Anyone could read an invitation incorrectly. She couldn't have been the first person in the history of the world to show up for a party on the wrong night. So that couldn't be the only reason for the whispers and the stares. There had to be more.

Well, there *was* more, wasn't there? After all, everyone probably knew by now that she'd also shown up for psych class an hour late. And maybe they'd heard about the TransAm, too. The car that no one but Cassidy Kirk had seen.

So it wasn't just the invitation they were whispering about. It was the whole picture.

And not a pretty picture at all.

It took all of her strength to dismiss the stares and whispers and concentrate on the game.

Sawyer and several of his friends arrived five minutes after the ball was put into play, but there was no room left in Cassidy's row. He shrugged, waved, and continued on up the bleachers, mouthing that he'd see her at halftime.

Cassidy didn't see Travis anywhere.

When Salem scored two touchdowns within minutes of each other, Cassidy's spirits lifted. The stares and whispers had been banished by the excitement of the game. She could relax and enjoy the game. It was a beautiful day, perfect football weather, she was with friends, and so far today, she hadn't messed up, big-time. So far.

Of course it was only the middle of the afternoon.

At halftime, the score was Salem University 16, State 0.

"Let's celebrate with a Coke and a hot dog," Sawyer said as he came up behind Cassidy. The stands had emptied the minute the gun went off, with everyone in a hurry to get to the refreshment stands before a long line formed. Talia and Sophie had gone with the crowd stampeding down the steps, but Cassidy had remained in her seat, waiting for Sawyer.

A few minutes later, she was leaning against the railing on the upper-level promenade waiting for her hot dog, when a girl named Tobie Shea from the dance committee approached, drink in hand.

"Hi, Cassidy," she said, leaning against the railing. She was short and heavyset, with beautiful dark eyes and long, straight black hair. Cassidy didn't know her well. Tobie seldom spoke up in psych class and seemed equally shy at the dance committee meetings.

But she seemed friendly enough now. "Great game, right?" she said, smiling.

Cassidy nodded. Her stomach rumbled. She hadn't had anything to eat, just coffee. Where was Sawyer with that hot dog?

"Listen, Cassidy," Tobie said, leaning forward slightly as if she suspected Cassidy might be hard-of-hearing, "I've been talking to a couple of people on the dance committee, and we were, well, we were wondering if you'd like one of us to take over as chairperson."

At first, Cassidy thought maybe she really *had* developed a hearing problem. She didn't see how she could have heard correctly. She had sold the idea as a fund-raiser, she had enlisted the aid of volunteers from psych class, she had made most of the arrangements. Of course she was chairperson.

"What?" she said, her eyes searching the crowd for some sign of Sawyer. She really was becoming faint with hunger. She should have eaten lunch instead of spending so much time wrestling with her hair. "What did you say, Tobie?"

Tobie raised her voice. "I *said*, we think someone else should take over as chairperson, Cassidy. Everyone's talking about how you came to class an hour late the other day and how you went to Nightmare Hall last night expecting a party. And then Noah heard some story about you and a car that no one else has ever seen." She began speaking faster, as if she wanted to get her unpleasant task over with quickly. "We figure, this dance is important to the mental health clinic, Cassidy, we've worked hard on it and," in a breathless rush of words, "wecan'taffordtohavesomeonescrewit-up."

Cassidy stared at the girl so intensely, Tobie's cheeks flushed scarlet. "You're kidding, right?" Cassidy said, her voice chilly. "You're not really suggesting I'm going to screw it up, are you?"

Tobie's eyes went to the cement floor and stayed there. "Well, not on purpose, Cassidy. But we all thought . . ."

"Who's we?" Cassidy interrupted.

"A few of us on the committee, we were just thinking maybe you have too much on your mind these days. I mean, you're working on other stuff, too, Cassidy, and there are classes and assignments and research and, well, we just thought you might be trying to do too much."

"Who?" Cassidy persisted. "Who is *we*?"

"Noah and Patsy and Nita and Roger and I."

Cassidy let out a small sigh of relief. Not Travis or Sawyer or Ann or Talia or Sophie. Not her friends. *They* hadn't betrayed her. That was something. In fact, that was a lot, considering the way her roommates had been looking at her this morning.

"I'm not a quitter, Tobie," Cassidy said, with far more conviction than she felt. Because although she didn't want to think it, it had occurred to her that maybe they were right. Noah and Patsy and Nita and Roger and Tobie. Maybe they were. Maybe chairing the dance was too big a job for someone who went to classes that were already over and parties that hadn't even started. "But you can go back and tell your friends that the minute I think my brain is turning to slush, I'll hand the reins over to someone else, okay?"

Tobie raised round, innocent eyes to meet Cassidy's. "But that's just it, Cassidy. Don't you remember what we learned in psych class? Professor Bruin said that in many cases of illusions and hallucinations, the patient is . . ."

". . . completely unaware of what is happening," Cassidy finished. "Yes, I remember. What's that got to do with me?" She hated the way her voice sounded. Defensive and hard-edged.

Tobie obviously hated it, too, and backed down. Acknowledging defeat, she said, "Nothing, I guess. It's just . . . well, if you change your mind, let us know, okay, Cassidy?"

"I won't change my mind."

Shaking her head, Tobie left.

When Sawyer arrived with Cassidy's hot dog, she was still thinking about the statement Dr. Bruin had made in class. "In many cases of mental illness, when the mind begins to disintegrate, the patient is completely unaware of what is happening." And there was more. She had continued, "There is total denial on the part of the patient, which makes proper treatment difficult, if not impossible, in the early stages."

Total denial? Well, of course. You'd have to be crazy to willingly admit that your brain was turning to yogurt.

As Sawyer handed her a mustard packet and a napkin, Cassidy laughed softly, bitterly, at her own choice of words. "You'd have to be crazy" to admit it? Wasn't it the other way around, according to Dr. Bruin? If you admitted that you might be going crazy, then you probably weren't, and there was hope for you. But if you denied it . . .

If you denied it, there probably *was* something wrong.

Wasn't that exactly what Tobie had been hinting?

Chapter 11

Salem beat their archrival, State University, by twelve points. Spirits were high as the crowd pushed its way out of the stadium.

Cassidy hadn't gone back to her seat after halftime, sitting instead in the top row of bleachers with Sawyer. She didn't think Sophie and Talia had minded. Maybe they'd even been relieved that she hadn't returned. They couldn't have been all that happy about the stares and whispers.

By the time Sawyer and his friends and Cassidy had made their way down the steps and emerged from the stadium, Talia and Sophie were long gone. Cassidy felt a little lost. Sawyer was so busy doing a play-by-play of the game with his pals that he hardly seemed to notice she was there. Deep in conversation, he didn't see the car when Cassidy did.

She had just rounded a corner of the high

stone wall surrounding the stadium when she spotted the TransAm. Her heart stopped. She saw the car clearly, in spite of the dense crowd in front of her. It was parked across the street, between a yellow pickup truck and a white Mercedes-Benz convertible. And the driver was inside. The dark window glass hid his face, but small puffs of white smoke from the exhaust told her the engine was idling. He had to be behind the wheel. Watching *her*?

The sight of the car filled her with dread. But she quickly realized that she should be rejoicing that it was there, right in front of her. Because she wasn't alone this time. Sawyer and his friends would see it, too, and soon everyone would know that her imagination wasn't on overdrive, after all. Word would spread quickly that Cassidy Kirk's brain wasn't self-destructing. Sawyer could testify that there really was such a car on campus, no matter what the registration records might say.

But before she could call out to Sawyer, there was a sudden surge forward in the crowd and Cassidy was swept along with it, away from him. When she glanced frantically over her shoulder, she saw that he was still lost in conversation with his friends. He hadn't even noticed that she was no longer with them.

Fighting to halt her forward rush, she called,

"Sawyer, look! The car, it's across the street! Sawyer!"

He didn't hear her over the noise of the jubilant crowd.

And although she continued to shout at him to look, she knew she might as well have been whispering for all the good it was doing.

The crowd continued to sweep her along.

By the time Sawyer caught up with her at the curb, the TransAm was gone, its place already filled by a motorcycle. Cassidy had to fight to hold back tears of disappointment.

"Why didn't you look?" she shouted at a stunned Sawyer. "The car was there, right there," she said, pointing, "and I wanted you to see it so you'd know I wasn't crazy! But you didn't pay any attention!"

"I don't think you're crazy," he said slowly, taking her hand, clearly puzzled by her reaction. "But," he glanced across the street, "where exactly *was* it? I mean, there doesn't seem to be room over there for another car."

"Well, not *now*," she said in disgust. "The motorcycle just parked there. But there *was* room. And the TransAm was there." She couldn't believe she'd missed her opportunity to prove that she wasn't seeing things. "I wanted you to *see* it!" she cried in frustration. "So you'd know it really exists."

"I told you," he said patiently, leading her across the street, "if you say you saw it, then you did. I'm sorry I wasn't paying attention, Cassidy, but it's no big deal. Why are you so upset?"

I'm *upset*, she thought angrily, because this was my chance to prove that I'm not losing it, and you weren't paying attention. Knowing that wasn't fair, she said aloud, "The car upsets me. I think he's following me. Watching me. And I don't why."

"Maybe you should talk to the campus police," Sawyer suggested as they made their way across the campus under huge old elm and maple trees with multicolored leaves.

"And tell them I'm being haunted by a black TransAm? How can I? According to your friend Tom, there's no such vehicle on Salem's campus. That's the first thing the police would check, and when they found out what you found out, they'd be as convinced that I'm inventing the car as everyone else is."

"Maybe not. But I guess it would be hard to convince them. Without proof, I mean."

Cassidy couldn't disagree with that. And she couldn't stand to talk about the TransAm. What was the point? They walked in silence to the Quad, where Sawyer said suddenly, "Saw you talking to Tobie Shea." The sun had gone down and the air was turning rapidly colder. People who had been celebrating on the commons were giving up to take refuge inside. "You didn't look very happy. Was she giving you a hard time about something?"

"Not really." She wasn't going to share *that* conversation with anyone, not even Sawyer. "She had a few complaints about the dance committee, that's all. No big deal."

He accepted that explanation. Telling her they'd all decided to go to Johnny's Place, a club in town, to celebrate, and that he'd pick her up at eight, he left her at the door.

Everyone in 56A was going into town. Sophie and Talia had dates, and Ann was meeting Travis there. She announced this cautiously when she arrived home from baby-sitting, as if she were expecting Cassidy to react unpleasantly to the news.

"Great!" Cassidy said cheerfully as she slipped into a short, red leather skirt and matching sweater. "So we all have dates tonight. That makes life just about perfect, doesn't it?" She pulled on thigh-high black boots. "It wouldn't be any fun going to Johnny's Place alone. Trust me. I went to a *party* alone, and I got the wrong night."

Ann laughed uncertainly. "Well, it's nice that you can joke about it."

126

Yeah, isn't it, Cassidy thought sarcastically. How many choices do I have?

"You sure you have your inhaler?" Sophie asked as they left for the lobby to meet their dates.

"Yes, I have it," Cassidy responded sharply. "Do *you* have your key, which you are constantly forgetting, Sophie Green?"

Sophie laughed and, not offended at all, turned back to the room to retrieve her key.

"Now, which one of us is it that needs a keeper, Sophie?" Cassidy asked slyly as Sophie rejoined the group.

"Me," Sophie said, laughing again, "it's me, Cassidy. And thanks for reminding me about my key."

Forgiving her, Cassidy said, "And thanks for reminding me about my inhaler. Really."

"Really," Ann echoed, smiling at Sophie as they entered the lobby. "I was there when Cassidy had that attack. It was horrible. Even with her inhaler. I don't want to think about what an asthma attack would sound like and look like if she didn't have that thing handy." Ann shuddered. "I hope I never have to see that."

"You won't," Cassidy assured her flatly. "I promise."

"At least it's a physical condition," Talia said, "not a mental one. You're lucky there's medication for what ails you, so to speak, right?"

"Right," Cassidy said, but by then they were in the lobby, and Cassidy forgot about asthma entirely because Sawyer looked terrific in a blue sweater that matched his eyes.

He almost ruined the evening before it began by asking her, "You feeling okay?"

But she told herself that people asked that question of other people all the time, and it didn't mean anything. It didn't mean that Sawyer had joined the ranks of those who were suddenly questioning Cassidy Kirk's mental stability. It just meant that he cared about her, that was all. Nothing wrong with that. Nothing at all.

"I'm feeling great!" she said, smiling up at him. "Just great. Let's party!"

The road to town was filled with cars honking their horns in triumph over Salem's win and people shouting out of car windows. The mood at the club would be one of jubilation. Should be a lot of fun, Cassidy told herself as they pulled into the parking lot in front of the long, low warehouse-style building.

But as they approached the doorway, she suddenly felt uneasy. Please, she prayed as they went inside, please don't let anything weird happen tonight.

The plea surprised her. She hadn't been this

nervous since she was five years old. What was different about tonight? She was with friends, she was a good dancer, and she always had fun at Johnny's Place.

No! She was going to have a great time tonight. If anyone stared at her or whispered about her actually showing up on the right night, she would give them such a look, their bones would dissolve. And nothing, absolutely *nothing* weird was going to happen. She wouldn't allow it.

And for quite a while, it didn't.

She danced with Sawyer. And she danced with Travis, while Ann watched from the sidelines, pretending to be talking to Tobie Shea, but looking as if she'd just tasted something nasty.

I never knew she was so possessive, Cassidy thought, surprised. Ann had always seemed so calm, so cool, not at all the kind of person who would keep a tight rein on her dates.

It was just like Dr. Bruin said in psych class. You never knew what was going on underneath someone's exterior behavior. Cassidy's mother had phrased it differently, saying, "Don't judge a book by its cover," but it meant the same thing. It meant that you had to know people a long time before you *really* knew them.

She had thought that she knew Travis and

Ann really well. Wrong on both counts. Maybe Ann was actually as demanding as Travis. In that case, they should get along perfectly. A match made in heaven.

"The music's great, isn't it?" Travis asked as the song ended. "So, is it all set for Misstery to play at our dance?"

Cassidy nodded. "But I need to talk to Lola about the details. Maybe I can do that tonight."

So, when the band took a break, Cassidy signaled to Lola to join them at their table. She seemed grateful for the opportunity to sit for a few minutes, and gratefully accepted the cold drink Sawyer handed her. "It's hot under those lights," she complained, yanking her long, blonde hair high up on her head and fastening it with a clip. "I should be used to it, but I'm not."

"You guys are great," Cassidy said, meaning it. "And it's really nice of you to waive your fee for our dance."

Lola took a long, deep swallow of her drink, sat the cup down on the checkered tablecloth, and looked at Cassidy. "Dance? What dance?"

Chapter 12

Two or three separate converations had been taking place around the crowded table. When Lola said, "Dance? What dance?", everyone stopped talking at once. An apprehensive silence descended upon the group like a dark cloud.

Cassidy laughed nervously. "Very funny, Lola. As if you didn't know. The dance we're giving for the mental health clinic. Two weeks from tonight."

"Two weeks from tonight," Lola said emphatically, "we're playing at a high school dance in Juniper, about an hour from here. We signed the contract yesterday afternoon."

The silence at the table thickened, became ominous.

Cassidy cleared her throat. "No, Lola, that's not possible. You must have your dates mixed up. Remember, I wrote you about our dance.

And you sent back a confirmation. I have it in my room."

Lola laughed. She reached up and brushed back a sweaty lock of hair from her face. "Cassidy, I don't sit down and write formal notes of acceptance. I'm a musician. I don't even own any stationery. We do everything by phone. A quick call, a yes or no, and then we sit down with the client and sign a contract. I never signed a contract with you. And I don't remember getting any letter from you, either."

Cluching at straws, Cassidy said desperately, "Don't you read your mail?"

"Of course. I read all of it." Lola grinned. "Just in case some big recording company is writing us with an offer. And I'd remember if there'd been a letter from your group, Cassidy. There wasn't. If there had been, I wouldn't have just blown it off. That's not the way we operate. I'd have called you. There *was* no letter."

Shock and dismay had rendered Cassidy speechless. She could think of nothing else to say. Lola seemed so certain.

As everyone stared at her accusingly, Cassidy thought, No, no, this isn't happening. I wrote that letter. I did! And Lola wrote back to me.

"I have the confirmation letter in my room," she said softly.

"Well, if you do," Lola said, standing up, "it's not from me. Sorry about the dance. Wish I could help, but we can't be in two places at once, can we? Let me know how it goes. Gotta get back to work now. Have fun." The fringe on her suede vest swung as she walked back to the bandstand.

Cassidy stared after Lola's departing back. Have fun? Impossible now. Everyone at the table was staring at her with looks that ranged from disappointment to undisguised disgust.

"We were counting on Misstery to draw a big crowd," Travis said.

Ann nodded. "It's just not going to be the same without them. Besides, I told everyone they were going to *be* there. Good thing we hadn't put up any posters yet."

"Well, we've already sold a lot of tickets," Sophie said. "I don't think people will cancel and want their money back just because Misstery isn't going to be there. We'll get another band."

"Where?" Talia asked. "It's late. If a band is any good at all, it'll already be booked for two weeks from tonight."

"Well, we can't have a dance without a

band," Sawyer pointed out. "We'll have to find someone."

"Or hire a deejay," Ann said gloomily. "No one's going to like that very much. A dance with black-and-silver decorations and candles on the table should have live music."

Cassidy listened to all of this with growing misery. No one had said aloud, "How could you mess up like this, Cassidy?" But she knew they were all thinking it. "I can show you the letter of confirmation from Misstery," she said defiantly. "It's in my desk."

No one nodded or said, "Sure, of course you can, Cassidy. We believe you."

"And I'll get another band," she added quickly.

"No, that's okay," Ann said hastily, "I'll do it."

Now, everyone nodded. Their eyes avoided Cassidy's as their heads bobbed up and down enthusiastically.

The nods were every bit as insulting as open accusations would have been. Her friends no longer trusted her.

She *had* to show them that letter of confirmation from Misstery.

As if the atmosphere at the table wasn't depressing enough, a few minutes later, Tobie Shea came by with her date in tow. She stood behind Ann's chair, opposite Cassidy, her eyes suspicious. "Something's going on," she said flatly. "You guys all look like you just got suspended from school. What's wrong?"

Before Cassidy could stop her, Ann was spilling the whole, dismal story.

"Okay, that does it!" Tobie said, surprising Cassidy with her vehemence. She no longer seemed the least bit quiet or shy. "I'm calling a meeting next week to find a new chairperson. I know you guys don't want to replace Cassidy, because she's your friend, but this dance is important and we need someone in charge who knows what she's doing." And she stormed off, dragging her embarrassed date with her.

"Don't worry about it, Cassidy," Sophie said after a moment of painful silence. "We outnumber Tobie and her friends. You're not going to be replaced."

"Maybe I should be," Cassidy said quietly, and got up and ran from the table, taking refuge in the rest room.

It was small, and crowded. She stood at the sink, staring into the mirror at a pale, bewildered face. What was happening to her? How could so many things go wrong so quickly? She had worked so hard to prove that she was capable, competent, healthy . . . no longer the sick, frail patient she'd been when she was little. And now it was all going wrong.

A tall, thin girl with dark hair in a French braid stood at the companion sink, talking over her shoulder to a friend. "There's so much going on right now," she said, applying eye shadow as she talked. "There's the party next Friday night at Nightmare Hall; that should be a blast."

Cassidy winced. Unlike her, *this* girl knew her social calendar.

"And then," the girl continued, "the freshmen psych majors are putting on a great dance the following weekend. Sam North asked me. The basketball player? He's so cute. And Misstery is playing, so I wouldn't miss it for the world. I can't wait!"

Cassidy felt sick. She turned and bolted from the restroom.

When she returned to the table, everyone was getting up, ready to leave. Their festive mood had been banished by Lola's announcement.

That was fine with Cassidy. All she wanted to do was get back to her room and find that confirmation letter from the musical group. She was sure she'd put it in her desk.

But then, she thought as Sawyer took her hand and led her from the club, I've been sure of a lot of things lately, and I've been wrong about all of them.

She was relieved that no one felt like stopping anywhere to eat. They were back at the Quad in fifteen minutes.

Cassidy's heart was pounding wildly as they approached 56A. She had said nothing about hunting for the confirmation letter. It would be too humiliating to let them know how desperate she was to prove herself right.

Of course, the minute she went to the desk and began fumbling around inside, they'd all know what she was up to. But then she'd find the letter, and she'd show it to them, and it would be okay. Misstery still wouldn't be playing at the dance, and that was a problem, but at least they'd all know she'd been telling the truth about the letter.

She made an effort to appear casual as she moved to the desk. Sophie and Talia went downstairs to get drinks for all, Travis and Sawyer sprawled on the carpet, and Ann lounged on her bed. Sawyer attempted to make conversation, but it fell flat. Their elation over the football win had completely dissipated, replaced by gloom.

Cassidy's fingers moved quickly through the array of papers in her desk. Tuition and bookstore receipts, notebooks, the invitation from

Nightmare Hall, photos, tons of notes from classes, old essays, charge card carbons . . . piles and piles of papers accumulated during the first few months of school.

When her fingers failed to come in contact with anything that felt like Lola's letter, she bent over the desk, head down, and began searching in earnest, glancing up only once, to find Sawyer's eyes on her in sympathy. He knew exactly what she was searching for. But there was something else in his eyes, something that rocked Cassidy to her core. Doubt.

There was doubt in Sawyer's eyes as he watched her frantic movements at the desk. Sawyer didn't expect her to find the letter. Because he didn't believe it existed. That hurt so deeply, Cassidy felt as if someone had just plunged a knife into her chest.

Still, she kept looking. It was here, it *had* to be here. She'd find it. Then she could whip it out of the desk, hold it up high, let them all see it. Let them all see that she wasn't losing her grip, that she knew what she was talking about, that she wasn't seeing things.

When Sophie and Talia returned with the drinks, Cassidy was still searching, her head bent over the desk, her hands tossing papers left and right. She didn't realize she was muttering to herself until Sophie said uneasily,

"Cassidy, who are you talking to?"

Cassidy raised her head. They were all staring at her. Sophie's face was worried, and the concern in Sawyer's eyes had deepened.

And Cassidy realized how it must look. There she was, bent over the desk, tossing papers this way and that, muttering to herself like a maniac, her fingers flying frantically in an effort to find something no one believed she'd ever possessed.

No wonder they were all staring at her as if she'd just stepped off a spacecraft and antennae were sprouting over her ears.

"It's not here," she said, softly, giving up. "The letter from Lola. It *was* here, but it isn't now. Someone must have taken it."

But she knew without asking that no one in the room believed there had ever been a letter.

Chapter 13

Cassidy knew she should just forget about the letter. There was no way to prove that she'd ever had it. And freaking out about it was just making things worse. But something in her refused to admit defeat.

"Lola signed it," she said as she left the desk and sat down on the bed, hands folded in her lap. "She did. The letter said that because the dance was a benefit for the mental health clinic, Misstery would waive their fee. I was thrilled, because that meant we'd save a lot of money."

"It's weird that you didn't tell us that," Ann said. "I'd think you would have told everyone."

"I forgot. I got busy and I forgot," Cassidy said defiantly. She had meant to tell them, it was such good news. But then something else had happened and the letter had flown right out of her mind.

Out of the *hole* in her mind?

Her head ached. "It was such a nice letter," she said almost dreamily, staring down at her fingers. She noticed that the pink nail polish was chipped on the little finger of her left hand. It looked gross. She would have to fix that, first chance she got. "For a musician, Lola writes a very nice letter."

No one said anything.

Cassidy lifted her head. "Maybe it's in your room, Sophie," she said. "Maybe it got mixed in with your mail after I opened it. I think you should go look."

Sophie and Ann exchanged a weary glance.

"Give it up, Cassidy," Talia said. "Even if you found the letter now, Misstery is already scheduled to play somewhere else the night of the dance. We'll find another group to play."

"I think I know someone who might be able to get us a great group," Ann said quickly. "Tobie Shea is a friend of Cal Donner, the lead singer for Tattoo."

Cassidy's upper lip curled in distaste. "Tattoo? They're a rock group. Strictly rock. They wouldn't play a slow, romantic song if you held a gun to their heads."

"You're exaggerating." Ann glanced around at the other faces in the room. "Isn't she?"

"No, she's not," Talia said heavily. "She's right. Tattoo is okay, but not for the kind of dance we're having. Their sound just doesn't go with black and silver, candles and flowers."

"Well, it's not like we have a lot of choices on such short notice," Ann snapped.

"Hey," Sawyer said, "this isn't a meeting of the dance committee, okay? We can talk about this stuff tomorrow. Sophie, put some music on. I'd like to relax a little before I call it a night."

Cassidy stood up. Suddenly, she couldn't stand the sight of any of them. They all thought her brain was turning to spaghetti. And they made her think that, too. "I think we should call it a night right now," she said, her voice flat and emotionless. "Travis, we've got that bike ride tomorrow. If we're too tired, we won't be able to keep up with everyone else." She had no intention of going on that bike ride, but if she admitted that now, they'd all want to know why. Sophie would ask her if she was sick.

She wasn't sick. But everyone in the Hike and Bike Club would stare at her, whisper about her, expect her to do something weird or stupid. They'd be watching her, waiting to see what might happen. She couldn't stand that. It would make her so nervous, she probably *would* do something weird.

Travis would just have to find out tomorrow

that she wasn't pedaling up the hill to the state park with the rest of the club. He could handle it. It wasn't like he still cared whether or not Cassidy Kirk was around.

No one argued with her about leaving. They were all tired. It had been a long day, and it hadn't ended that well.

Besides, Cassidy thought when she returned to the room after kissing Sawyer good night out in the hall, I make them all uncomfortable. They'd never admit that, but it's true.

Well, that's okay, she told herself as she crawled into bed, because I make *myself* uncomfortable.

She had been physically ill a lot as a child. And she hadn't liked it. But that was nothing compared to the sheer terror she felt now, thinking there might be something wrong with her *mind*. Her pills wouldn't help, and neither would her inhaler.

What would become of her if her mind got sick?

She didn't get out of bed the next morning. When Ann asked if she was awake and wanted to go to breakfast, Cassidy didn't answer. And when, as the three were leaving the room, Sophie called out a reminder about the bike ride, Cassidy remained silent, burrowed deep in the blankets, facing the wall.

She stayed in bed all morning, and was still there when her roommates left again, this time for lunch.

"She's going to be late for the bike ride," she heard Sophie say as they left. Then the door closed behind them and Cassidy had the room all to herself.

There wasn't anything she wanted to do with the peace and quiet but sleep. Deep, blissful sleep, that was all she wanted. That wasn't so much to ask, was it?

Apparently, it was, because a short while later, someone began pounding on the door to her room and shouting her name.

Travis.

He had come to *collect* her? He was crazier than she was.

"You're not going to sleep your life away!" he called from beyond the door. "Open the door or I'll break it down."

Yeah, right. The guy was a runner, not a weight lifter. But he was making so much noise, he'd draw a crowd if she didn't shut him up.

Throwing aside the covers in disgust, Cassidy padded to the door and yanked it open. "Are you nuts?" she hissed. "Can't a person sleep around here?"

"Not all day," he said cheerfully. He was

wearing blue bicycle shorts and a blue tank top under a Salem windbreaker. His white plastic helmet was in his hand. "Time to go. Throw some clothes on, and make it quick. We're already late."

"*I'm* not late. Because I'm not going. So trot along, Travis, and give the hikers and bikers my regrets."

He stood firm. "Nope. You committed yourself to this ride, and you're going. Unless, of course," raising one eyebrow, "you'd rather they all speculated as to why you didn't show up. I'm sure the reasons they'd invent would be far more imaginative than the truth, which is that you just chickened out."

Cassidy hesitated. She knew he was right. She had helped start this group on campus, and she'd talked a whole bunch of people into joining. Everyone was expecting her. If she didn't show up, rumors would be flying thick and fast across campus tomorrow morning about how she'd hidden in her room all day instead of taking the planned bike trip.

The news about Misstery not playing at the dance was already on tap for tomorrow's rumor du jour. Wasn't that enough? Did she really want to provide even more material for the rumor mill?

No. She didn't.

"I'll be right there," she told Travis and slammed the door in his face. She'd go, but she didn't have to be pleasant about it.

It took her less than ten minutes to don red bike shorts, a matching long-sleeved top, and a white sweater. She was tying the laces on her white sneakers when Travis rapped on the door again. "Get a move on," he called. "Post time is three minutes from now."

Making sure she had her inhaler and her key, Cassidy filled her water bottle, grabbed her fanny pack, and left the room.

She refused to speak to Travis. She had the uncomfortable feeling that he'd been ambushed by her roommates. He'd probably had no more interest in collecting her for the bike ride than she had in going, but they'd persuaded him that she needed to get out of the room, then talked him into being the one to "rescue" her.

She just hoped it hadn't been Ann who had talked him into it. That would be too much.

Before she hopped on her bike, she checked the back tire. It seemed fine. Bless Sophie! She'd taken it to the shop, after all. Sawyer was right. Delegating responsibilities was a good idea. On the off chance that anyone should ever again *give* her any responsibility, which didn't seem likely now, she'd have to remember that.

The group was just leaving the administration building when Travis and Cassidy arrived. She was grateful that they were bringing up the rear, which eliminated the stares she'd been dreading.

They rode to the park along the river path behind campus, the clear, rushing river on one side, the woods on their right. It was another beautiful day, cool but sunny, with a bright blue, cloudless sky overhead. It took less than a mile of riding for Cassidy to be grateful that Travis had dragged her out of bed. She would have spent the entire day worrying herself sick if it hadn't been for him.

She glanced across at him, riding beside her on the dirt path. "Travis?"

He turned his head. "What?"

"Thanks."

"You're welcome." He smiled at her then, and it no longer mattered to Cassidy that he probably had been bullied into dragging her forth into the sunshine. That seemed unimportant, even if it *had* been Ann's doing.

They were forced to take a detour when a small bridge over a waterfall proved to be unsafe. A large orange sign tacked to the railing made it clear that they would be riding over it at their own risk.

As a result, they arrived at the state park

later than anticipated. No one seemed to care. On such a gorgeous day, counting minutes seemed foolish.

But the delay meant that by the time they left the park, the sun was already beginning to sink in the west. They were going back by the main road, and now they would have to ride in traffic after dark.

Cassidy hated to leave. She had forgotten how much fun Travis could be, at least when things were going his way. They had explored the woods, taking a long break to sit by one of the larger waterfalls and talk, and they had even made each other laugh.

If only he wasn't so demanding.

It did seem pretty ironic, though, that they'd broken up because she was too busy. If things kept going the way they'd been going, before too long, she wouldn't be busy at all. No one would trust her to be in charge of anything.

She wondered, as they walked back to the clearing where they'd parked their bikes, how Travis would react if she said, "You know, Travis, if you'd just hung around a little while longer, I could have devoted myself totally to you, because there isn't going to *be* anything else in my life."

He'd probably say something like, "Yeah, but who wants a basket case for a girlfriend?"

Anyway, he had Ann now.

By the time they were halfway between the park and school, darkness was falling rapidly, swallowing up the woods on either side of the road. Every bike had the required light and reflectors, and there was very little traffic. But Cassidy missed the sunshine and the daylight. Riding wasn't as much fun at night, and it was getting very cold.

It was Travis who started the argument. They were pedalling up the road in the dark, some distance behind the rest of the group, when he said suddenly, "So, you couldn't talk Duncan into becoming a pedal-pusher?"

Cassidy frowned. Why was he bringing up Sawyer? She hadn't asked *him* about Ann. "No. He's too busy. But *I* don't mind," she added pointedly, "because I'm busy, too. That's the way we like it. We give each other plenty of space. And I don't see Ann Ataska anywhere around here, either."

"We're not joined at the hip," Travis said sharply.

"Oh? I thought that was what you wanted." She was angry with him for ruining what had been a really nice time. And even angrier with herself for caring that he had ruined it. "I thought you wanted someone to adore you every second of the day."

149

Travis made a sound of disgust low in his throat, stomped down on his pedals, and raced away. He kept pedalling furiously, and the distance between them widened rapidly. Cassidy watched in dismay as the beam from his bike light, shining on the road, grew further and further away.

She was alone in the darkness, with nothing but silent, black woods on either side of her.

The blood in her veins began to race. There was no moon overhead, no streetlights along the road. Only the tiny light on the front of her bike, providing illumination as she pedalled as fast as she could to catch up to the group. They must have gone around a curve just then, because she could no longer see the little pools of reflected light on the road up ahead.

She pedalled faster, although her chest was beginning to ache. How could Travis leave her out here alone like this? Sawyer wouldn't have. Never.

There *was* a curve. She whizzed around it, and had just emerged on the straightaway when her rear tire began thumping ominously and the bicycle began to drag heavily against her pedalling.

Oh, no. Sophie, Cassidy screamed silently, you promised!

The bikers up ahead disappeared around another curve.

She couldn't keep riding with a flat tire. As much as she hated the idea of stopping on the pitch-black road, Cassidy knew she had no choice. Travis would notice, eventually, that she wasn't catching up with them, and he'd come back for her. She had to climb down, before the tire was ruined beyond repair. Maybe it already was.

She slowed, stopped, climbed down, her breath coming in short, rapid gasps. Her parents had been dead set against Cassidy biking, saying it would be too much of a strain. Only when the new medication proved so beneficial had they allowed her to buy the racer.

Now, she thought maybe they'd been right. The ride had been too long and she'd been pedalling too fast in an effort to catch up to the others. Her chest hurt, and she could feel a coughing spasm coming on. Great. That was all she needed now. Just the thing to make her misery complete.

She reached into her fanny pack for her inhaler. As she bent her head, she saw the faint glow of headlights behind her, coming very slowly around the curve she'd just rounded.

Forgetting the inhaler, she straightened up. The car was headed toward campus. She'd hitch a ride. They could put her bike in the trunk, leaving the lid open. Or they could tie it to the roof. Then she could get out of this cold darkness and ride back to campus in safety and comfort. She wouldn't even wave to Travis when the car passed the bikers. Let him worry about where she was. It would serve him right.

She stepped out into the road and began waving her arms as the car came out of the curve.

At the very last second, as the oncoming headlights blinded her, it occurred to Cassidy that jumping into a car without finding out first who was behind the wheel probably wasn't such a hot idea. Struck by uncertainty, she darted to the opposite side of the road, in an effort to get a look at the car. Impossible to see it behind those blinding headlights, but she told herself the chances were good that it was someone from school, since it was headed toward campus. They'd take her with them and this dismal bike ride would become just an unpleasant memory.

Wrong.

She saw the dangling hearts first. Then the dark, tinted window glass, and then the black bulk itself registered. The TransAm.

As her breath caught in her chest, the car gunned its engine and, with a squeal of tires, sped up the road and raced straight toward the disabled bicycle.

Cassidy cried out.

The car slammed into the bike with a clash of metal on metal. The racer flew up into the air. The fat, round light on the handlebars was torn free on impact and flung sideways, landing in pieces at Cassidy's feet. A chunk of glass bounced off the highway and hit her in her shin. She cried out again, this time in pain, but never took her eyes off the bicycle as it sailed up into the dark night like a large red-and-silver kite, somersaulting once before it disappeared into the deep, thick woods and landed, unseen, with a muffled thunking sound.

Chapter 14

The realization that only moments before, she had been sitting *on* the bicycle that had just somersaulted into the air and crashed in the woods took Cassidy's breath away. If the TransAm had come along before the tire went flat, would it have swept bicycle *and* rider off the road in one blow?

"Thank you, Sophie," Cassidy whispered gratefully. "If you'd remembered to get the tire fixed, I might be dead now." That thought was so stunning, her knees gave, and she sank to the asphalt, wincing in pain as the rough surface scraped against her skin. But her eyes, open wide, remained fixed on the car.

It had come to a screeching halt after impact and sat now, directly opposite Cassidy, its engine purring, spitting its cotton-ball puffs of smoke from the exhaust.

"Go away!" Cassidy screamed. "Go *away!*"

The car honked once in reply, then drove away at a leisurely pace, as if it were out for a pleasant Sunday-afternoon drive.

The arrogance of its deliberate crawl infuriated Cassidy. She jumped to her feet, shaking her fists at the car. "Why are you *doing* this?" she screamed. "Why?"

Slowly, smoothly, the TransAm silently disappeared around the second curve.

It was dark on the road again. Empty. Silent.

Cassidy had never felt so alone. She would never forgive Travis for abandoning her. If it hadn't been for him, she wouldn't have come on this trip. And then he'd gone off, just because she'd made a nasty comment, and left her all alone on a dark road. Never mind that he couldn't have known she'd be at the mercy of a hit-and-run driver. He still shouldn't have left her.

Cassidy glanced around her. She was afraid to move, terrified of walking up the road only to encounter the TransAm again. But she couldn't stay where she was. It wasn't safe here, either.

Where *was* it safe?

Nowhere.

She knew she wasn't going to try to find the bike. It could have landed anywhere in those woods, and she had no flashlight. Even if she found it, she didn't have the strength to drag a crumpled pile of metal all the way back to campus.

Taking a deep breath, she set off down the road on foot, anxiously glancing around for any sign of the TransAm as she hiked. She walked on the berm for what seemed a very long time, and had just passed the second curve when she saw a faint light coming toward her.

Her heart began to pound furiously. The TransAm? Coming back to finish the job?

No. The arc of light on the highway was too small.

A bicycle.

Finally! Someone from the club had realized that one of their riders was missing.

Although her breathing had become painfully ragged, Cassidy picked up her pace. Anxious to reach the approaching bicycle, she broke into an unsteady lope.

Her steps slowed when she recognized the rider.

Travis.

"Where have you been!" he shouted when he reached her. "I thought you were right behind me, and . . . where's your bike?"

More than one sarcastic reply sprang to Cassidy's lips. But she was too shaken to spar with

Travis. "In the woods," she said instead. "A car hit it. It's totalled, I think."

He jumped off his bike. "A car? What car? Are you okay?"

"Yes, I'm fine. I wasn't *on* it at the time. I had a flat tire, so I stopped, and then . . ." She couldn't go over it all again.

Travis glanced around. "Cassidy, there hasn't been any traffic on this road for the last hour. Anything that passed you would have had to pass me, too. Nothing has. Not a single car."

Cassidy's stomach somersaulted. Not again. It wasn't happening again.

No. No, that wasn't possible. The car had *been* there, of course it had, and it had hit her bike. She couldn't be wrong about that. "Well, there must be a side road then," she said uncertainly. How could Travis not have seen the car? "A turnoff somewhere between where I was and where you were. Because my bicycle is lying in the woods somewhere back there, probably smashed to smithereens. If you don't believe me, come on, give me a lift and I'll show you."

When she was seated behind him, her arms around his waist, and they were on their way, she said into his neck, "It was the TransAm, Travis. From the car wash. Remember? The guy that gave me all that money?"

"The money that disappeared," he said bluntly over his shoulder.

Ignoring that, Cassidy said, "I saw it. It slammed into my bicycle, sent it flying into the woods, and then drove away slowly, as if it had all the time in the world. The guy, whoever he is, is totally psychotic!"

When Travis didn't answer, Cassidy realized that his helmet, combined with the whooshing sound of the wind as they rode, had kept him from hearing her.

She decided that was okay with her. He'd be more likely to believe her after he'd seen the bike, anyway. It was there, waiting in the woods, ready to prove to one and all that it really had been struck by a car. There were probably traces of black paint from the TransAm on it somewhere. She would call the police this time. What the driver had done was a crime, and he wasn't going to get away with it.

She recognized the spot immediately. It was exactly halfway between the two sharp curves. As they approached it, she tugged at Travis's sleeve, signalling him to stop. She climbed down behind Travis and tugged her helmet off. Then she turned to check once more to make sure they were in the right spot.

The first thing she noticed was that there was no glass anywhere on the road. Although her leg still stung and the small cut was surrounded by dried blood, the glass from her bike light had disappeared. There wasn't a trace of it on the asphalt. Not a trace.

And then she realized that Travis was staring at something lying on the berm of the road. "Cassidy?" he said in an odd voice. "What did you say happened to your bike?"

Even before she moved to join him, she saw it. Lying peacefully by the side of the road, as if it had been carefully placed there by loving hands. Red. Silver. Black, padded seat. Not a scratch on it anywhere. Round, silver light, completely intact, nestled securely on the handlebars.

"That's not mine," Cassidy said, as a sickening bewilderment swept over her. She moved closer to the bicycle. "It can't be. No way."

Travis reached down and plucked the water bottle from its holder. He held it up in front of her as she arrived at his side. "Your initials," he said bluntly. "C.K. That's you, right?"

"This can't be my bike," she repeated through stiff lips. "Mine is in the woods, probably wrecked. I *saw* it happen." But when she reached Travis's side, she saw the chip in the left pedal where she'd run into a cement curb last summer. "No," she said softly, "no, this is not possible."

Travis turned to look at her. He was frowning, his lips tight. "What's going on?" he asked.

"He *hit* it!" she cried. "I saw him hit it. I was over there." She pointed a trembling finger. "And my bike was here, on the berm, and the TransAm came around the curve and sent it flying up into the air. All I could think about was, if the tire hadn't been flat, I'd have been on it when he hit it and I'd have gone flying into the air, too."

"Cassidy."

"What?"

"The tire isn't flat. Sophie had it fixed, she told me she did. Look at it. It's not flat."

Cassidy looked. He was right. There was nothing wrong with the rear tire.

She couldn't bear the look on Travis's face. "But I . . ."

"Just get on it," he said wearily, "and we'll get going, okay? It's late. I'm beat." And he turned away to walk back to his own bike.

"Travis!" Cassidy cried, anguish in her voice because it was, after all, happening again. The same now-you-see-it, now-you-don't that had happened before. She couldn't stand it. Not again. It was like falling into a deep, black hole that never stopped. "It happened, Travis!" She was screaming now. "I didn't imagine it, I didn't!"

"I don't know what's going on, Cassidy," he said as he climbed on his bike, "but I think you need some rest. I know I do. Let's go."

He began pedalling away again. Terrified of being left alone a second time, Cassidy picked up the bike that couldn't possibly be hers but looked and felt exactly like it and got on. She began pedalling after Travis, her legs moving automatically, while her mind struggled frantically to make sense of the past hour.

How could this possibly be her bicycle? It *looked* like her bike, and it even *felt* like her bike, and there was that chip in the pedal. But . . .

Travis didn't believe her. She couldn't blame him. She had said her bicycle was in the woods, and it wasn't. She had said it was totalled, and it wasn't. She had said the tire was flat, and it wasn't.

Travis was only thinking what any sane person would think, under the circumstances.

Any *sane* person.

Does that let *me* out? she wondered. She felt like she was sinking into quicksand. Something awful had happened back there on the highway and now it looked as if it hadn't happened at all, and she didn't understand that.

They rode, single file, all the way to school in silence.

When Travis left her at the Quad, he said only, "Get some sleep."

His prescription for a nervous breakdown, apparently. Dr. Travis McVey, noted shrink.

She locked her bike in the rack, and ran into the building.

Sophie was sitting on Ann's bed, reading. She looked up when Cassidy burst into the room. "Whoa! Who's chasing *you*? How was your bike ride? You're so late. How can you ride in the dark? I'd be nervous . . . Cassidy? What's wrong?"

Cassidy had collapsed on her bed as if she'd run all the way from the state park. "Nothing. Nothing's wrong." She was very, very cold. Wrapping the comforter around her, she said, "Sophie, how much do I owe you for the bike repairs?" because she was hoping and praying that Sophie would say, Oh, gee, Cassidy, I'm sorry, I forgot to take your bike in. How did you ride with a flat tire?

Because if Sophie said that, wouldn't that mean the whole horrible business with the TransAm really had happened? Wouldn't that mean that she had *had* had a flat tire, and she had stopped on the highway, and the car had come around the curve and sent her bike flying into the air . . .

But Sophie didn't say that. What Sophie said was, "It was only two dollars, Cassidy. Don't worry about it. They never charge very much at the bike shop."

Pulling the flowered comforter more tightly around her, Cassidy began to tremble with cold and confusion and fear. But she wasn't ready to give up. Not yet. She couldn't. It was too hard to give up. Too painful. "Do you have the receipt?"

Sophie looked startled. "Oh, yeah, sure. It's here somewhere." She jumped off the bed and went into her own room. She was back a moment later with a messy handful of papers. But several minutes of rifling through them left her looking perplexed. "Well, it should be in here," she said. "I know this is where I put it." She glanced up from the papers. "Honestly, Cassidy, forget the two dollars, okay? You can buy me lunch this week."

"It's not the money," Cassidy said, knowing she should drop the subject. The quicksand tugged at her feet, threatening to swallow her up. But she couldn't stop now. She had so many questions. Why couldn't Sophie answer them for her? What kind of friend was she? "It's . . . well, the tire felt a little flat, that's all, and so

I thought maybe you'd forgotten to have it fixed."

"It went flat? Gee, I'm sorry. They must not have done a very good job patching the leak. But they *did* patch it, Cassidy. I didn't forget to take the bike in." Sophie thought for a minute and then asked, "If your tire went flat, how did you get home?"

The quicksand tugged harder. "Well . . . it wasn't as flat as I thought it was," Cassidy said lamely.

When Sophie gave her a questioning look, Cassidy got up and went into the bathroom. She never should have brought up the subject of the bicycle.

When she came out of the bathroom, ready for bed, Sophie glanced up again. "You okay, Cassidy? You look a little weird. Maybe that bike ride was too much for you. I mean, with your asthma and all."

"I'm not an invalid, Sophie." Actually, her body seemed to be doing just fine, even after the long, strenuous day it had had. It was her mind that was malfunctioning. And that was so much worse. "I'm just a little tired. All I want to do is sleep."

Sophie took the hint. She picked up her book, and headed for her own room. In the doorway, she said, "Oh, by the way, Sawyer called. I think he was worried. Because it was getting late and you weren't back yet. You should probably call him."

"Too tired," Cassidy murmured. And the thought of trying to explain something to Sawyer that she didn't understand herself was exhausting. Tomorrow . . . she'd be able to think more clearly tomorrow.

Then again, maybe she wouldn't.

What if she was never able to think clearly again, ever, in her whole life?

The thought filled her with raw, icy terror.

In psych class the following morning, Cassidy, pale and tired, listened with growing uneasiness as Professor Bruin talked at length about "breaking points for the human mind." I don't want to listen to this, Cassidy thought. Her hands felt like ice. She couldn't seem to get warm these days, no matter how many clothes she wore.

"Stress can weaken even the strongest among us," the professor lectured. "There are documented cases of hallucinations caused solely by stress. No drugs were involved, no hypnosis, and no diagnosed mental illness."

Cassidy turned her head just then and found Travis looking directly at her.

Are you okay? he mouthed silently.

Yes, she mouthed back, hating his concern for her.

But she knew she was lying. She was far from okay. She wouldn't be okay until she knew exactly how close to the brink of insanity she was dancing.

But she wasn't giving up without a fight. After class, she called Sawyer's friend Tom at the administration building and asked him for a favor.

"I'm doing a survey," she told him. "Do you think you could run the car registrations of all the faculty for me?" It had occurred to her, in one of her more lucid moments that morning, that if the car existed, it could belong to a faculty member. Sawyer had only asked Tom to check the students' registrations. She was reaching, she knew. Why on earth would a teacher be tormenting her? Maybe grasping at straws was what people did when they thought they were losing their minds.

"And we are looking for what, exactly?" he asked affably.

"The same thing we were looking for among the student population. A black TransAm."

"What is it with that car?" he asked. "You got a thing for black sports cars?"

But she could hear him clicking keys as he

talked and knew he was doing what she'd asked.

She held her breath. Please, please, she prayed.

"Nope," Tom said a few minutes later. "We got your Mercedes-Benzes, we got your Chevys and your Fords and a couple of motorcycles and a Jeep and two pickup trucks. But no TransAm."

"Are you sure?" she pressed, disappointment slashing at her like a razor blade.

"Cassidy, I know what I'm doing here."

"Well, could you try the employees, then? You know, the maintenance staff and the cafeteria and dining hall workers and the administration building clerks. Please?" She wondered if he could hear the frantic desperation in her voice. Probably. Now he'd believe the rumors about her.

He sighed, but the keys began clicking again. She waited.

"Sorry," he said finally. "As far as I can tell, there is no black TransAm anywhere on this campus."

Chapter 15

That afternoon, Cassidy was replaced as chair-person of the dance committee.

She didn't even argue about it. Although her cheeks burned when the result of the vote, which Tobie Shea had insisted upon, was announced, and although she wanted nothing more than to slide from her chair to the floor where no one could see her, Cassidy didn't argue. They were right to worry about how she would perform her duties. How could someone who was having trouble distinguishing reality from fantasy accomplish everything necessary for this dance?

Mentally, she reviewed the evidence: There *was* no black TransAm on campus. Her bike was safely locked in the rack in front of the Quad, and it didn't have a scratch on it. The cut on her leg was minor, and could have come from underbrush in the park and not a shattered bicycle light. The crisp new bills from the car wash had disappeared. Likewise, the essay she thought she'd given Travis. The invitation to the party at Nightmare Hall had the correct date on it, and there was nothing wrong with her clock or her wristwatch.

When you added it all up, as Tobie Shea obviously had, it meant there had to be something wrong with Cassidy Kirk's mind.

So she didn't protest when she was replaced.

After the dance committee meeting, Ann, the new chairperson via a second vote, walked to the back of the room to sit down beside Cassidy. "Since you've already ordered the decorations," she said, her voice maddeningly gentle, "you can still be in charge of those, okay?"

"Gee, thanks, Ann," Cassidy said, unable to resist the sarcasm. "I am truly honored."

Ann looked hurt. "Cassidy! It's not my fault. Listen, I didn't vote against you. None of your friends did. But Tobie had more people on her side than we thought. And they were determined to replace you."

What was the point of arguing now? Hadn't she already decided they were right to replace her? "Never mind," Cassidy said, standing up as Travis walked over to join them. "Forget it, Ann. You'll make a great chairperson. Good luck." And without glancing Travis's way, she hurried from the room.

She went for a long walk along the river-bank, reluctant to return to the Quad. They would probably all go there after the meeting in the library basement was over. She didn't want to see any of them.

It was a cool, cloudy day. The river was high, babbling furiously as it rushed along between its banks. Cassidy sat on a fat, gray rock over-looking the water, her head on her bended knees, thinking about how quickly she had gone from loving every moment of college life to dreading getting up in the morning. How had that happened? *Why* was it happening?

"Not thinking about jumping, are you?" a voice said in her ear, startling her.

Sawyer. "Been looking for you," he said, sitting down beside her. "I heard about what happened yesterday."

"You and everyone else on campus," she said, staring out over the water. "And you're being tactful, Sawyer. What you really mean is, you heard about what I *said* happened but probably didn't. Am I right? You heard about a car that wasn't there, a tire that wasn't really flat, and a bicycle that wasn't really smashed to bits, right?"

"Travis said you'd be upset if I mentioned

it. But I just thought maybe we should talk about it."

Travis had said she would be upset? Well, Travis ought to know. He'd been there when the whole thing happened, seen how upset she was when they found her bicycle lying by the side of the road in one piece. If only he'd seen the black TransAm, too . . .

"Maybe you had an accident," Sawyer suggested. "On your bike. Fell and hit your head, and the whole car thing was kind of a dream, while you were unconscious."

Cassidy knew he was trying to be helpful. "Sawyer, I'd *know* if I'd had an accident."

The expression on his face told her he wasn't so sure. She could tell he didn't know what to make of this new Cassidy. When he'd met her, she had been strong and confident and busy. Like him. That Cassidy wouldn't have been sitting on a rock staring at the river. She had never had time, for one thing. Too many other things to do.

It wasn't the kind of thing Sawyer would do, either. Finding her here must have been a surprise to him. Or maybe not. Maybe nothing she did now surprised anyone.

Sawyer thought she'd had an accident and then forgotten about it? Cassidy sighed in despair. When her friends thought she was seeing a car that wasn't there, they decided she was going off the deep end. But when she refused to invent an accident that she was pretty sure *hadn't* happened, Sawyer questioned that, too. She couldn't win.

Was anyone ever going to believe her again?

"Look, don't worry about it," he said, reaching for her hand. "You probably just need a good night's sleep, that's all. Maybe the ride was too much for you, with your asthma and all. Dr. Duncan orders rest, and plenty of it."

When he put his arms around her and kissed her, she felt like a patient being given a shot. Therapy. Sawyer's kiss felt like therapy. Like he was hoping it would cure her.

She hated that. Hated that he thought she *needed* a cure.

And the worst part about that was, he was probably right.

When she returned to the room later, the door was standing open, and she could hear voices inside. She'd been right about their coming back here after the meeting.

Her stomach began to churn. The last thing in the world she wanted now was to walk into a room full of people. Especially people who knew she was no longer chairperson of the dance committee.

But Sawyer had been right about one thing.

She *was* tired. She wanted to lie down, hide in her bed, snuggle down under the covers the way she had as a child. Maybe she wouldn't get up until the semester was over. That seemed like a good idea.

She'd throw them all out, and then she'd crawl into bed. It was *her* room.

She was almost to the doorway when she heard Travis's voice say, "I told her all along that if she didn't slow down, she was going to self-destruct. She wouldn't listen. That's what split us up. But I was right, wasn't I? I'm telling you, she's on the edge. One more push and . . ."

Ann interrupted him. "I agree with Travis. It started with that essay she said she'd given him when she really hadn't, and it just got worse from that point on. It makes me nervous, living with someone who sees things that aren't there. Who knows what she'll do next?"

Sophie's voice followed. "I've always envied Cassidy. She was so organized, so efficient, and she seemed to have so much fun getting things done. Not at all like me. I know she didn't believe I got her bike tire fixed, and I don't blame her. It's just the sort of thing I'd forget. But I *didn't* forget. So how could she have had a flat tire yesterday?"

"She didn't," Travis said. "I saw the tire. It

was fine. And there never was a car out there, like she said. I would have seen it."

"One of us could talk to our parents," Ann said. "They're all experts. But Cassidy got so upset when Talia suggested that she talk to Talia's mother."

"It's weird," Talia said. "Cassidy seems like the last person in the world to lose it like this. I guess we could talk to Professor Bruin," she suggested then. "She's a psychiatrist. She could probably tell us what to do."

Cassidy's face felt like it was on fire as she stepped into the room, catching them all by surprise. "You don't need to go to Professor Bruin," she said heatedly to chagrined faces, "because *I* can tell you what to do. You can get out of my room. If there's anything I *don't* need right now, it's a bunch of amateur psychologists discussing me. I want you all to leave."

"This is my room, too, Cassidy," Ann said quietly.

"So, you stay. But the next time you want to have a meeting to discuss my sanity, I'd appreciate it if you'd conduct it somewhere else. Maybe at the mental health clinic in town. That would be more appropriate, wouldn't it?"

"Cassidy," Sophie said pleadingly, "don't be mad. We're just worried about you, that's all."

"Right," Cassidy snapped, and moved past them into the bathroom. She slammed the door as hard as she could, and leaned against the edge of the sink, fighting angry tears.

How *could* they? How could they talk about her behind her back like that? Practically dissecting her, as if she were a frog in science lab.

She wasn't some stupid science project!

Knowing how they all felt, there was only one way she could stay on campus now. If she wasn't willing to pack her bags and grab the next bus back home, and she *wasn't*, she would just have to be extra, extra careful not to see things that weren't there. And if she *did* see something weird, or something strange happened, she would just have to keep it to herself. She would share it with no one, not Ann or Sophie or Talia or Travis, not even Sawyer. He'd want to believe her, but she'd see the doubt in his eyes. And that would hurt.

No, if she was going to make it at Salem, she was going to have to work really hard at appearing to be as sane as anyone else on campus.

She laughed bitterly to herself. Was it possible to *act* sane if you weren't? She really should ask Professor Bruin.

Cassidy turned then and stared at herself in the mirror over the sink. "You can't ask Professor Bruin if it's possible to fake sanity," she told herself softly. "Because the answer might be no. And then where will you be?"

When she returned to her room, it was empty. Voices from Sophie and Talia's room told her Ann had probably been unwilling to face her, and had retreated with them. Or maybe that was Talia talking on the phone to her mother-the-shrink, begging her for advice.

Cassidy sank into the comfort of her bed gratefully, and was asleep in seconds.

All that week, she felt as if she were walking on eggs. When she crossed campus, she kept her eyes on the ground, fearful of seeing the black TransAm. Equally afraid of saying something that would raise eyebrows, she kept quiet in class. After classes, she went directly to the library, sitting in a dark corner until late. She ate alone, from the vending machines in the Quad's basement, and went back to her room only when she was sure that everyone was either asleep or out. And she slept as much as possible, going to bed early, getting up late if she had no early-morning classes.

Sophie and Talia both tried to talk to her. "We miss you at dinner," Sophie complained on Wednesday. "You can't be studying every single minute. Everyone knows you don't need to. You never did before. Aren't you ever going to have fun again, Cassidy?"

Talia was more sympathetic. "I don't blame you," she said as she waited for her date on Thursday evening. Cassidy was already in bed, saying she had a headache. She didn't, but if Talia kept talking, she would.

"I know how horrible it must be, being stared and pointed at and talked about," Talia continued. "You must hate it. But if you keep this up, people are going to really wonder about you. You *are* going to the party at Nightmare Hall, aren't you? It's tomorrow night. My mother says you have to show up, because it's the only way to prove to everyone that you're okay."

So Talia *had* called her mother.

"I'm not going anywhere," Cassidy muttered, pulling the comforter up underneath her chin.

Talia hurried over to sit on Cassidy's bed. "You have to go, Cassidy! Don't you get it? It'll show everyone you're a good sport, that you've got your act together enough to just blow off the mistake you made when you showed up on the wrong night. No big deal. It's the only way. You know I'm right."

"Go away, Dr. Talia, I'm not interested in your amateur headshrinking. Besides, I already went to a party at Nightmare Hall, remember? I didn't have fun."

Talia gave up.

Cassidy meant what she'd said. She had no intention of walking up the steps to Nightmare Hall on Friday night.

But on Friday morning, in psych class, Travis raised his hand when Professor Bruin had finished her lecture.

"Yes, Mr. McVey?"

"I was wondering . . . we've been talking a lot about stress causing hallucinations under certain circumstances. If the hallucinating really is due to stress, what would the recommended treatment be?"

Cassidy swallowed hard. Was he talking about *her*? How could he, with her sitting right there?

"That's in the next chapter, Mr. McVey. We haven't touched on it yet. If you'd like to read ahead, feel free."

"Yeah, I will, but we were talking about this the other day, and someone suggested that maybe retreating from everyday life might be the answer. You know, giving up your usual activities, sleeping a lot, sort of hiding out, you might say. I said I didn't think that was the answer, and we kind of argued about it."

Cassidy fumed. They'd been talking about

her again? She hadn't come to any of them with any more wild stories, so why were they still discussing her? She raised her head and directed a contemptuous glance in Travis's direction, signalling him with her eyes to get a life.

He ignored her.

"Read the chapter, Mr. McVey. But in the meantime, you can tell your friend that if it were that simple, most of the population would be hiding in their rooms and psychiatrists and psychologists and counselors would be out of business."

Travis nodded knowingly.

Cassidy wished she were sitting close enough to slap his smug face.

She was hurrying to the library after class when he caught up with her. He grabbed her elbow and spun her around to face him. "So?" he demanded, "were you listening? Did you hear what Bruin said? It's not that simple. Hiding out won't do the trick."

She tore her elbow out of his grasp. "You think you know so much! You don't know anything! You sure as hell don't know anything about *me*! But I know something about *you*. The only reason you want me doing business as usual is, you're hoping I'll fall apart from stress, just so you can say you were right when we argued that last time. God, Travis, is it *that* important to you to be right?"

His mouth tightened and his dark eyes narrowed. "Did Sawyer tell you that? That I have some compulsive need to be right?"

"I *heard* you," Cassidy cried. "At the Quad the other day. You were in my room, and I heard you with my own ears."

He nodded grimly. "Like you saw with your own eyes a black car no one else has ever seen?"

Uttering a cry of exasperation, Cassidy turned and raced away to the library.

Travis didn't follow her.

But her tormented mind made a decision as she ran across campus under the huge old trees, almost bare now of leaves. She had to go to the party at Nightmare Hall. She *had* to.

The discomfort of showing up, the stares, the whispers, would all be worth it, just to see the look on Travis McVey's face.

Hiding out, was she? Well, she'd show him.

She was going to that party.

If it was the last thing she ever did.

Chapter 16

Sophie, busy scrunching her wet hair in front
of the dresser mirror, was delighted when she
learned that Cassidy had changed her mind
about the party. "That's great! You sure you
feel up to it? You've been so tired lately."

Cassidy feigned an old woman's voice.
"Well," she cackled, "I think I can drag these
old bones to one more outing before I give up
the ghost."

Sophie laughed. "You *are* feeling better."

Not true. Not true at all. Cassidy felt as if
she were trying to hold her brain together with
her bare hands.

But Sophie didn't need to know that Cassidy
was going to Nightmare Hall to prove a point.

Determined to do a good job of convincing
everyone just how fit she really was, she spent
two hours on her hair and makeup and her outfit. Black suede jeans and a red silk blouse,

black suede vest and boots. Nothing sickly about that.

"You look fantastic!" Talia said admiringly. "I'm glad you took my advice. I mean, my mother's. But it's mine, too. Staying home would look like weakness, and you're not weak, Cassidy."

Make that *wasn't* weak, Cassidy thought bleakly. Past tense.

Ann came in then, and stopped short when she saw the way Cassidy was dressed. "I thought you weren't going to the party."

"I'm the one who talked her into it," Talia boasted.

For just one fleeting moment, Ann's face registered surprise and . . . disappointment? Annoyance? Cassidy couldn't be sure. Whatever it was, it wasn't delight.

But Ann recovered quickly, forcing a smile and saying heartily, "Well, good work, Talia. Your powers of persuasion are impressive."

"Not really," Cassidy said casually. "Since I'm feeling fine, I didn't have any excuse not to go. I wouldn't want to be rude and not show up without a reason."

She half-expected Ann to retort, "A nervous breakdown is a perfectly good excuse, Cassidy." Ann said instead, "Well, I'm glad you're going. It'll be fun."

But it wasn't. At least, not for Cassidy Kirk. She thought at first it might be. The house was much more brightly lit than it had been last Friday night, and crowded with partygoers. Cassidy had mixed feelings about that. On the one hand, she wanted everyone to notice that she was there and feeling fine. At the same time, she was seized by a strong desire to blend into the crowd and go unnoticed. So that no one would stare at her or whisper about her. With so many people, that could happen, couldn't it?

It didn't. Three times, she walked into a room and people stopped talking. The sudden, heavy silence gave them away. They'd been talking. About *her*.

Then Sawyer never showed up. "He thought you weren't coming," Sophie said accusingly. "You should have called and told him you'd changed your mind. Why didn't you?"

Cassidy didn't know. Something to do with that last therapeutic kiss, she supposed. Or maybe it was because her sole purpose in coming to this party had been to show Travis and everyone else that she was fine. Just fine.

She didn't need Sawyer for that.

Travis was with Ann, who seemed to Cassidy to be keeping a very tight leash on him. He did manage to elude her once halfway through the evening. Suddenly, Travis was at her side, asking if she was having a good time.

"I'm having a wonderful time," she said, her tone of voice just a shade too cheerful. "It's much more fun to go to a party at Nightmare Hall when they're actually having a party." She held up a cracker. "They even have food this time."

Travis laughed.

"I'm dying of thirst, though," she said, feeling suddenly self-conscious. There wasn't as much triumph involved in fooling Travis into believing she was fine as she'd thought there'd be. He didn't seem all that surprised that she'd shown up. Did that mean he'd known all along she could pull herself together for this party? Sawyer hadn't, or he'd be here. "I need something cold to drink."

"I'll get it," he offered, and she let him.

He was returning, a can of soda in hand, when Ann reappeared. For the second time that day, Cassidy noticed the expression on her roommate's face. When Ann saw Travis approaching Cassidy, holding out the can of soda to her, her cheekbones went white and her hands, dangling at her sides, curled into tight fists.

"Hey, Ann," Cassidy called recklessly, "come on over and have a seat! Travis was just wondering where you were, weren't you, Travis?"

And although Ann's expression relaxed then, and she hurried over to them, Travis shot Cassidy a look of annoyance.

Oh, well, can't win 'em all, she thought, wondering at the same time why Travis would resent someone telling Ann he'd been missing her.

Folding one hand over Travis's left arm, Ann said to Cassidy, "Just for your information, the restrooms have Salem University stickers on the doors. That's so we won't go wandering into someone's room by mistake. This is a dorm, after all, although it's so different from the Quad, it really doesn't feel like it. Anyway, there's a restroom downstairs, off the kitchen, and two more upstairs."

"Thanks." Cassidy took a healthy swig of her ice-cold soda. "And thanks, Travis, for the drink. You're a lifesaver."

Tom Lucas, Sawyer's friend from the administration building, came and asked her to dance then. She plopped her soda can on a windowsill and followed him out of the room. She was very careful to smile confidently at every party guest who stared at her as she walked to the dance floor.

Let them stare. She was here and she looked

great and if she wasn't having the best time she'd ever had, they couldn't know that. She had no intention of letting it show.

She danced to three fast numbers in a row with Tom. They were both very good, and by the second number, people had cleared the floor to watch them. The onlookers clapped their hands in time to the music as Cassidy and Tom danced up a storm.

"So, where's Sawyer?" Tom called over the music and the clapping.

She shook her head and shrugged.

"You ever find that car you were looking for?" he asked as she twirled under his raised arm.

"No." She didn't want to talk about any of that stuff now. She was dancing, and people were watching, but not because they thought she was weird or crazy, they were watching because they thought she was a good dancer. For the first time in a long while, she felt . . . *normal*. She didn't want that ruined by thoughts of the phantom TransAm.

By the end of the third dance, she was beginning to wheeze a little. If there was one thing she didn't want tonight, it was an asthma attack. It would defeat her whole purpose for coming to this party . . . to show everyone how together Cassidy Kirk was.

She thanked Tom for the dances, excused herself, and hurried back to the front parlor where she'd left her drink.

The room was empty, but her soda can was still on the windowsill.

Breathing hard, Cassidy snatched it up and drank.

By the time she realized that her hand around the can was not cold, as it should have been, but uncomfortably warm, it was too late. She had already taken a long gulp from the can.

And although she spat immediately, trying to escape the burning hot liquid as it poured from the can, her lips, mouth, and throat were already on fire.

Cassidy screamed in pain, dropped the can, and ran from the room.

Chapter 17

Hand to her burning mouth, Cassidy raced along the hall's hardwood floor, past the library, past the dining room, pushing her way through startled clusters of party guests gathered outside each room, until she got to the kitchen. It was crowded with people, all of whom stared as she rushed into the room and glanced about wildly for the nearest source of cold water.

She was only vaguely conscious of Travis and Ann, Talia and Sophie, standing with Milo Keith, Jess Vogt, and Ian Banion, all of them watching in awe as she dashed toward the sink.

Silence fell quickly, as if someone had suddenly pulled the plug on a radio. All eyes in the room were on her as she grabbed an empty paper cup from the counter and thrust it under the cold water faucet. Filling the cup, she gulped water down, her hands shaking so hard half the contents spilled over her blouse and vest.

But the water salved her burned lips and tongue and soothed her seared throat.

"What's going on?" Sophie's voice said from behind Cassidy.

"Cassidy, what's the matter?" Ann asked impatiently as they all began to gather around the sink. Talia was busy shooing everyone else out of the kitchen, something Cassidy would have appreciated if she hadn't been frantically trying to douse the fire in her mouth and throat with cold water.

When she finally felt some relief, she turned away from the sink, leaning against it, the cup still in her hand. Water dripped down her chin and wet spots covered her silk blouse and suede vest.

"That wasn't a case of simple thirst," Travis said. "What's wrong?"

It was hard to talk. Her lips hurt. "Someone," she began unsteadily, "someone put steaming hot coffee in my Coke can."

The long, disbelieving silence hurt almost as much as the hot liquid had.

Cassidy looked at Travis, hoping for some support. "That Coke you brought me, remember? I put it on the windowsill when I went to dance. When I came back, it was still there, right where I'd left it. But instead of cold soda, there was boiling hot coffee in it. I found out the hard way, by drinking it!" She grabbed a paper towel from the roll beside the sink, and dabbed at her lips with it. "I think I'm getting blisters."

Ann peered closely at Cassidy's face. "I don't see anything. You look fine to me."

Cassidy gingerly licked her lips. "It still hurts. The coffee must have gone straight from the coffeemaker into the soda can."

Still no one said anything.

Cassidy felt her cheeks grow as hot as her lips had been only moments before. "You don't believe me, do you?" she accused. "Well, I'll prove it to you. Wait here, and I'll go get the can. The coffee will still be in there. I hardly drank any." Before anyone could protest, she ran from the room.

The front parlor was no longer empty. People holding paper plates on their laps had taken seats around the room. But the Coke can was still on the floor, right where Cassidy had dropped it. A pool of liquid surrounded it, soaking into the carpet.

Ignoring the stares of everyone in the room, Cassidy bent and scooped up the can. "Mustn't litter," she said lightly, and can in hand, turned to go back to the kitchen.

But she realized immediately that something about the can wasn't right. Something was different. She hadn't been in the kitchen that long. The can should still be warm. But it wasn't. It was, in fact, cold.

She left the parlor slowly, her steps hesitant. Why wasn't the can still warm? That coffee had been too hot to cool off so quickly. Even if she'd been gone longer than she thought, it would still be lukewarm. It would not, however, be as cold as what her fingers were now touching.

Unwilling to continue toward the kitchen until she was sure, Cassidy leaned against the wall in the hall and held the can up in front of her, touching here, touching there, with her fingers, hoping to feel some small shred of warmth.

It was cold all over. Nothing warm, nothing hot, had been inside this can recently.

I picked up the wrong can, that's all, she told herself, moving back to the parlor to glance quickly inside. There had to be another can. Someone must have come in and picked up her can and put it somewhere.

Oh, sure, a little voice in her head said sarcastically, and then they dropped a different can on the floor in exactly the same spot, just to balance things out, right?

There were no other discarded soda cans anywhere in the room.

The one she had in her hand, the one she had scooped up off the floor, had to be the same can she had dropped earlier.

But now it contained nothing but the dregs of cold soda.

I won't go back to the kitchen, she thought, conscious of a painful tightening in her chest. I can't face them. I'll just leave now, walk back to campus alone or hop a shuttle. No one will even know I'm gone.

"Did you find it?" Talia's voice said.

Too late. No escape now. Cassidy turned around. Talia was standing in front of her, an inquisitive look on her face. "Is that the can?" she asked.

Without answering, Cassidy brushed past her and led the way back to the kitchen. "I know what you're all going to say," she announced grimly, "and I guess I can't blame you." She held the can aloft. "There is nothing in this can now but cold soda. All I can tell you is, when I drank from it a few minutes ago, it was filled with scalding hot coffee, and I burned my throat and my lips and my tongue."

Into the awkward silence that followed, Sawyer's voice said, "Cassidy? What's going on?"

He was standing in the kitchen doorway. "I called over here to see how the party was going, and Ian told me you were here. I decided to catch up with you. How come you didn't tell me you'd changed your mind?" As he walked into the room, he picked up on the highly charged atmosphere and repeated, "What's happening?"

Cassidy glanced around at the faces surrounding her. They were blank. They were obviously trying very hard not to register disbelief. She could almost see them struggling to pretend that nothing weird was going on.

It was hopeless. She could spend the rest of the night explaining what had happened to her in the parlor, but with only cold soda in the can now, her words would be wasted.

Icy, metal bands tightened around her chest.

"Nothing," Cassidy told Sawyer. "Nothing at all. I'm glad you're here. But listen, why don't you all go back to the party while I see what I can do about these disgusting water spots on my vest? I'll just be a minute, Sawyer. Wait for me on the dance floor, okay?"

"You sure you're all right?" Travis asked, as Ann tugged on his sleeve.

It took every ounce of will Cassidy possessed to say in a normal tone of voice, "Of course! Go dance with Ann like a nice date, Travis. I'm going to get one more drink of water." Her head high, she turned her back on all of them and walked to the sink again. Over the sound of running water, she heard voices muttering in disagreement.

But when she turned around again a few minutes later, the kitchen was empty.

Cassidy leaned against the sink, grateful to find herself alone. She directed a hostile glance toward the Coke can, sitting on the oval wooden table.

It couldn't have had hot coffee in it, she thought, moving to the table to pick up the can. Not possibly. It's cold. It was cold when Travis handed it to me, it was cold when I picked it up off the floor, and it's cold now.

Dr. Bruin had called the imagination a "very powerful tool." She had even said that in mental illness, many people used that imagination against themselves, sometimes in very bizarre ways. "Some people hear voices, sometimes entire conversations. Others see images that are so real to them, they can describe them down to the tiniest detail."

Compared to entire conversations and detailed images, hot coffee in a Coke can didn't seem like such a challenge for a vivid imagination.

What was the proper psychiatric term for

someone who believed they had burned their own lips and tongue and throat, actually *felt* the pain, when in fact, they hadn't done any such thing?

She didn't want to know what the proper psychiatric term was.

Just to be sure, she would check out her mouth very carefully in the restroom mirror. If, like Ann, she saw absolutely no evidence of any kind that her lips had been burned, she would have to give up and blame her imagination totally.

That was such a scary thought, her knees wobbled. And the pain in her chest increased.

Her fingers closed around the black velvet purse hanging by a golden chain on her left shoulder. She could feel the inhaler inside. Maybe I should use it while I'm in the rest room, she thought as she moved toward a door off to her right boasting a blood-red Salem University sticker. If the doctors are right about stress aggravating asthma, it's a miracle I'm not already stretched out on the floor tile wheezing like, as Ann would put it, a dying frog.

She pulled the inhaler from her unzipped purse with one hand while the other hand reached out, turned the doorknob, and pulled the stickered door open.

Because her eyes were focused on her purse, she didn't see that what she was stepping onto was not solid white squares of rest room floor tile, but instead a set of narrow, wooden steps leading downward, flanked by a wall hung with tools on one side and a rickety wooden railing on the other.

Still looking down into her purse, she pulled out the inhaler and was reaching out with her hand to locate a light switch when her foot came down hard. On nothing. Knocked off balance by the misstep, Cassidy pitched forward, head-first, letting out a small, startled cry as she sailed out into a cold, dark, musty cavern.

Chapter 18

As Cassidy slammed into the wall at the foot of the stairs, bounced off, and landed with a painful thud on the hard earthen floor, a sudden breeze sailed in through an open kitchen window and slammed the cellar door shut. The light from the kitchen above vanished abruptly, plunging the cellar into darkness.

After a long moment, Cassidy stirred and tried to pull herself upright. The door at the top of the stairs opened slowly, carefully. Cassidy raised her head, tried to call out, but the fall had knocked the wind out of her, and her voice along with it. She raised a hand in appeal, a silent gesture that clearly said, "Help me."

The door closed with the click of finality.

Completely disoriented, Cassidy didn't realize for several moments that she wasn't breathing normally. And that it wasn't just from the fall. She was severely allergic to mold and mildew, and she could smell both in this dark, chilly cavern. Still, the coughing took her by surprise when it welled up inside her chest and spilled out into the cellar, one wracking spasm after another, shaking her entire body.

She straightened up, hoping that would help.

It didn't. The coughing was out of control. She needed her inhaler.

Her hand went to her side in search of her shoulder bag.

It wasn't there.

The sound that came from Cassidy's throat was tortured, a loud, rasping sound that echoed throughout the musty space. She had to fight for every breath, as if someone had tightened a metal vise around her chest.

Gasping, unable to shout for help, she got on her hands and knees and began searching frantically in the darkness for the lifesaving inhaler. Above her, so *close* above her, she could hear party sounds . . . music, laughter, conversation . . . couldn't they *hear* the dreadful sounds she was making? So loud, like a power saw scraping across a thick tree limb, so loud, why couldn't they *hear*?

It was bad, this attack, the worst ever. Without the inhaler, she could die. That had been explained to her, more than once.

She knew it was true.

"Somebody help me," she tried to whisper, but the only sound she uttered was another loud, hoarse rasp.

Refusing to give up, she scrambled on hands and knees along the cold, earthen floor, her hands frantically sweeping its surface for the missing shoulder bag.

Above her, Travis and Ann entered the kitchen, leaving the party sounds behind. He went straight to the refrigerator for ice. "So, where'd you go?" he asked as he collected ice cubes.

"When?"

"A few minutes ago. I thought you were right there behind me, but when I turned to say something, you weren't there." Then he added drily, "That seems to be happening to me a lot lately."

"Oh, I was talking to Sophie about the dance. You know, the dance you haven't asked me to yet? We're a little worried about the decorations. I mean, the way Cassidy's been lately . . ."

"What was that noise?" Travis interrupted when he'd dropped the cubes into his cup.

Ann straightened the collar of her blue blouse. "What?"

"That noise. Didn't you hear it? Like a car with a bad battery. From the cellar?"

Ann laughed. "I didn't hear anything. Like there'd be a car in the basement, Trav. What's in your drink, anyway?"

Travis frowned. "No, I mean it. Listen!"

Smiling tolerantly, Ann obeyed. And her smile disappeared. "I hear it. God, what is it?" She listened more intently. "It sounds like . . ." She looked at Travis with wide eyes. "Travis, where's Cassidy?" she asked sharply.

"What?"

"She never came back inside, did she? And that sound coming from the cellar, it's horrible, but I've heard it before. I'll never forget it. I heard it for the first time that night Cassidy had her asthma attack at the Quad. Travis, that's the same sound."

Travis dropped his drink and ran to the cellar door, yanking it open. The rasping sound filled the staircase, echoing up and out into the kitchen. He reached out and flipped the light switch at the top of the stairs.

Cassidy was on her knees, her hands on the dirt floor. Her mouth was open and her lips, when she turned her face upward, had a faint bluish tinge.

"Call an ambulance!" Travis barked at Ann, and took the stairs three at a time.

Cassidy was unable to speak, but when Travis reached her, she gestured with her

out loud that she didn't know *what* she was seeing these days.

Easier to sleep and avoid everything.

But on Monday, she dressed and went to all of her classes, then to a dance committee meeting, a Hike and Bike Club meeting, and made a trip to the bookstore to buy notebooks. Her motions were automatic, her mind numb. Throughout the day, people asked her with what seemed like genuine concern how she was feeling, and she told them she was feeling fine. Look! she wanted to say, look how well I'm functioning, just like a normal person. But she couldn't eat, and she couldn't concentrate, and she was just going through the motions.

She knew she needed help. How much of her mind was left? How long would it take to lose the rest of it? Then what would she be? When the last of the real Cassidy Kirk had disappeared forever, where would they put the empty shell that was left? In the kind of hospital where Talia's mother worked?

The thought made her physically ill.

But while she was still functioning, she could at least pretend she was normal, and that meant finishing up the business of the decorations. Ann and Talia and Sophie had all asked her that morning, innocently enough, if everything was "taken care of," and she'd been asked again by others at the committee meeting. She knew they were all worried that she'd forgotten something.

She didn't think she had. But how could she be sure? The only way to know was to go to the mall and pick up the order.

Since she couldn't carry all of the supplies on her bike and it would be awkward on the shuttle, she drove. It felt good for a change. Driving was a competent act that required concentration. She seemed to be doing it okay. Hadn't driven off the road or crashed into another car. That was a good sign, wasn't it?

It was twilight by the time she pulled out of the campus parking lot, and already beginning to grow dark when she parked in front of the mall. She should have left school earlier. Ever since she'd nearly hit a deer driving home one night shortly after she got her license, she had hated driving in the dark.

But collecting the supplies was important. It would be worth a little night driving to see the expressions on everyone's faces when she dropped the decorations on her bed.

The mall was uncrowded, the rental-supply store empty but for the clerk.

When Cassidy told the woman why she was there, the clerk nodded, excused herself, and was back in minutes carrying two shopping bags filled to the brim, the surfaces covered with tissue paper.

"Could I just see the tablecloths, please?" Cassidy asked.

"Of course. I'm sure you'll love them." Bending, the woman pulled one tissue-wrapped parcel from the bag, laid it on the counter, and unfolded the covering. "There!" she said, "isn't that pretty!"

It was pretty. It was very pretty. The only problem was, the folded tablecloth Cassidy was staring at wasn't black.

It was royal blue.

"It's blue," she said in a dull voice. "That tablecloth is blue."

The woman looked up. "Well, yes, of course it is. They all are."

"I ordered black."

"Well, that was the first time," the clerk said patiently. "But then you called and changed the order to blue and orange. And I must say, the order was much easier to fill than the black and silver would have been."

Cassidy's stomach rolled over. Blue and orange? Those weren't even Salem's colors. "What are you talking about?" she asked, her voice rising. "I never changed the order."

The woman's smile disappeared. She reached into the bag and pulled out a slip of paper. "Here it is, right here," she said, her tone of voice decidedly less friendly. "You called a week ago and changed the order. I have your student I.D. number right here on the slip."

"But I *didn't*!" Cassidy cried. "I never called you! We wanted black and silver, and that's what I ordered. That's what I have to have! I *have* to!" She remembered then with sickening clarity that blue and orange were the school colors of their archrival, State University. How could she go back to campus with bags filled with blue and orange? "I can't *take* this stuff, I can't!"

"Well," the woman said coolly, rewrapping the offending blue in its tissue paper, "I just don't see any way that I could locate the black and silver at this late date."

Cassidy leaned forward over the glass case. "You have to! Oh, God, you *have* to!"

Hearing the panic in her voice, the woman's face softened. "Your dance is Saturday night?"

Cassidy nodded numbly.

"Well, I'll do the best I can. If I don't have any luck, could you use these instead?"

"Oh, no," Cassidy breathed, "absolutely not. No way."

"All right, then. I don't understand any of

this, but I'll do my best. Call me on Thursday. I'll know by then."

Dazed and shaken, Cassidy left the store. How could this have happened? Had she really called the woman and changed the order? Could she have done that without even knowing she was doing it? Was this just another part of what was wrong with her?

It's like some other part of me is deliberately trying to sabotage me, she thought dazedly as she made her way through the mall. A very *sick* part of me.

And what was she going to tell everyone when she got back to the dorm?

Nothing. She was going to tell them nothing. She would pray like crazy that the clerk managed to come up with the black and silver and if she didn't, there'd be time to face the music then. But not now. She was too tired. Too tired.

And scared. She had never been so scared. Something terrible was happening to her mind, and she didn't know what to do about it. Where was she to go for help? Who should she talk to?

She was crying quiet tears of despair as she drove past Nightmare Hall, thinking as she did so that the fall down the cellar stairs hadn't been as bad as this, this terrifying feeling that her brain was dissolving and she couldn't stop it from happening.

The tears blurred her vision. She reached with her right hand for a tissue just as something large and bulky darted out of the woods and into her path.

Cassidy screamed, stomped down on the brake, but too late.

There was a loud, sickening thunk and a body flew up into the air, somersaulted, and landed fifty feet away at the edge of the woods.

Chapter 19

As the car screeched to a halt, Cassidy's head snapped forward, slamming into the steering wheel. But not before she'd seen the body flying up into the air.

She didn't lift her head. She couldn't. Fully conscious, she was nevertheless too dazed with shock to move.

She struggled to think. She had hit something? Someone? Oh, no, no, not that. She couldn't have.

But she *had*. She had felt the impact, seen the . . . body . . .

Oh, God, no.

She should get out of the car. She should go look, see how bad it was.

She lifted her head. Something warm and sticky dripped down her cheek, teased the corner of her lip. She reached out tentatively with her tongue. Salty . . . but not tears. Blood. From her forehead.

She should get out. She should go look.

Had she *killed* someone?

No, no, she couldn't have. Couldn't have.

But she knew she could have.

She sat very still, her hands sitting limply on the wheel. She had to do something.

But she could not get out and look at that body. She could not.

Her hand reached up and threw the car into reverse, her foot came down hard on the accelerator, and in a spin of gravel and screeching tires, she raced backward until she reached the driveway to Nightmare Hall. Spun the wheel sharply right, tore up the driveway, stopped the car, jumped out, ran to the front door and began pounding with both fists, screaming for help.

Jess Vogt was the first to reach the door. Ian Banion was right behind her. "What on earth . . . ?" Jess cried when she saw Cassidy's tear-streaked face and blood streaming from a cut on her forehead. "Cassidy, what happened?"

"Come, come with me," Cassidy gasped, "in my car. Hit someone, I hit someone, on the highway, come with me, please, I can't look, I can't . . ."

Without asking any questions, Jess and Ian ran to the car with her, Jess taking the driver's seat, urging Cassidy into the front passenger seat, Ian in the back.

No one said a word.

"There!" Cassidy cried when they reached the spot, "it was right there. He's . . . he's lying there, at the edge of the woods. Is he dead? Go see if he's dead. Oh, God, please don't let him be dead."

"I'll check," Ian volunteered and jumped out, leaving the lights on so he could see.

The two girls sat frozen in the front seat, holding hands, as Ian's tall, lanky figure walked into the path of the lights.

He walked up the highway several hundred feet.

Then he turned around and walked back again, clearly searching the road and the edge of the woods with his eyes.

He shrugged as he turned to go over the same ground a second time.

"Why hasn't he found him?" Cassidy whispered. Her head was beginning to ache terribly. "He was right in front of me. I never saw a thing until it was too late."

"It wasn't your fault," Jess said soothingly. "I'm sure it wasn't. And maybe he wasn't even hurt badly, Cassidy."

"Oh, yes, he was. He had to be. He hit my car so hard, and then he flew up into the air . . . just like my bicycle, that night by the state park." Immediately she thought, I shouldn't have said that. No one believes that ever happened. I don't even believe it now.

Ian returned to the car, opened the door, got in, turned toward Cassidy. "I don't know what you hit, Cassidy, but it couldn't have been a person, or else they couldn't have been hurt. Because I looked up and down the highway twice, and didn't see a thing. There's no one there. No one at all."

Chapter 20

"No, Ian," Cassidy said, wringing her hands, "that's not right. That's not *right*! I hit him, the front of my car hit him and he flew . . . he has to be there, he *has* to!"

Ian shook his head. "Cassidy, I'm telling you, there's nothing there. Nothing. Not an animal, not a person, nothing. I wouldn't lie to you."

And Cassidy knew that. Everyone on campus knew that Ian Banion wouldn't lie.

It was too much. Too much. The terror of believing that she had killed or injured another human being had already sucked most of the life out of her. Now, the relief that she hadn't done that, after all, was so overwhelming, it drained the last bit of strength from her bones.

But the horrifying knowledge that something she had believed to be so real was just another hallucination was the most draining of all. All of those things combined sent her over the edge.

The wail of despair that came from her mouth then chilled Jess and Ian. They had expected Cassidy to be relieved by Ian's news. They stared in horror as instead, she hid behind her hands, deep, mournful sounds pouring out of her.

"Get her to the infirmary," Ian told Jess in a low, intense voice, *"now!"*

Cassidy's despairing wails continued as they raced up the highway to campus.

The doctor who cared for her was friendly and gentle. She bandaged Cassidy's forehead, gave her a pill to calm her down and then sat by her side until the medication took effect, saying there were two doctors on duty and no other patients.

"Your friends tell me you've had a rough time of it," the doctor said. Her plastic name tag read *Dr. Cleo Mandini, M.D.*

Cassidy turned her face away. Jess and Ian had talked about her to the doctor? Probably told this nice woman that Cassidy Kirk was a basket case, ready for a padded cell. Humiliating. It was so humiliating. But true. So true.

The pill was working. Her headache was going away, and there wasn't anything wrong with her breathing, in spite of the horror of what had just happened out on the highway. Or . . . *hadn't* happened. Whatever, Cassidy thought foggily, letting the medication begin to erase her anguish.

The doctor was still sitting beside her bed.

"I see things, you know," Cassidy said in a low, confidential tone. "Did they tell you? I see things that aren't there. Everyone knows it. I even know it. Don't you think that's funny, that I know it, too? I always thought . . . I always thought that when you hallucinate, you don't *know* that you did it. But *I* know. Does that mean I'm not as far gone as some people?"

"What kind of things do you see?" the doctor asked, patting Cassidy's hand.

Jess and Ian must have told her to check me out, Cassidy thought. She's going to play psychiatrist for me. Isn't that nice. God knows I need one. "Well," she said lazily, "I see essays that I didn't really write, and I see the wrong time on my clock and wristwatch, and I see the wrong date on invitations and I see money that isn't really there and I see stickers on doors and then there's this car . . . this car . . . the car is the worst. Only it doesn't really exist. I know, because I checked. It's only in my head."

"What kind of car is it?"

Nice of her to humor me, Cassidy thought. Well, why not? Maybe talking about the car would make it seem less real. "It's a TransAn.. Black. With dark, tinted windows that make it look like no one's driving it. And it has these cute little red hearts, two of them, tied to the driver's door handle."

The room was so white, so very white, there seemed to be white everywhere. And it was chilly. Maybe she wasn't really in the infirmary, after all. Maybe she was lying outside on the commons in the middle of a cold, white blizzard. Cassidy shivered and pulled the scratchy white blanket up under her chin.

And then Dr. Cleo Mandini, M.D., said so easily, so casually, as if she were saying that it just might rain tomorrow, "Oh, I know that car. It's not a figment of your imagination, though. It's very real. And it's right here on campus."

Chapter 21

"No," Cassidy said, "the TransAm isn't on campus. I checked the car registrations. Students,
faculty, and staff. No TransAm."

"That's because," the doctor said patiently,
"that car belongs to Pat Benham. Did belong
to him, I should say. He died, you know. Last
year. The best American history teacher we
ever had here, and the man grew the most
beautiful roses in this county. Cancer took him.
Left his wife with three small children."

Brenham. Three small children. The monsters Talia had talked about Ann baby-sitting?
Was there more than one Professor Brenham
on campus?

"Administration probably removed the car
from the computer after Pat died. That's why
you couldn't find it when you checked. His wife
doesn't drive standard transmission, and she
has a little compact car of her own, so she

wouldn't have updated the registration on the TransAm. Can't bear to sell it, though; Pat was so crazy about that car. It just sits in their garage. Every once in a while, she gets some student to take it for a spin, just to keep it in working order so she can sell it when she's ready."

Cassidy was struggling, through her drug-induced fog, to comprehend what the doctor was telling her. There really *was* a TransAm on campus? Black, with tinted glass and a pair of hearts dangling from the driver's door? There really was a car exactly like the one she'd seen?

Although comprehension was slow in coming, when it did come, it was stunning. *She had never hallucinated the car. It really did exist, and she really had seen it!*

She wasn't too foggy to understand the full implications of that one, astounding realization. It didn't end there. There was more, much more. She fought to sort it all out. If that car existed, then maybe her essay had existed, maybe the clock really had been an hour slow. Yes, that was possible. Probable, even. And the invitation really *had* had the wrong date on it when she opened it, she really *had* received the crisp new ten and twenties, the sticker really had been on the cellar door . . .

It went on and on.

"I'm not quite sure why you thought you had imagined the car," Dr. Mandini said. "Why would you think that?"

And the answer to that question came to Cassidy as if it were hanging in neon lights from the ceiling: *Because someone wanted me to think it. All of it. Everything. Someone wanted me to believe that I was losing my mind.*

"I don't know," she said softly. "It wasn't just the car. It was a lot of things." But it had been the incidents involving the car that had been the most frightening, the most devastating. Someone had been driving that car when it had terrified her. Someone who had access to it.

Who did she know who had access to the TransAm?

"Is there more than one Professor Benham on campus?" she asked, knowing that it was one of the most important questions she had ever asked anyone.

Dr. Mandini shook her head. "Nope. Just Leona. It's hard for her, raising those three kids alone. Pat was a terrific father, and I know those kids must miss him terribly. Leona has baby-sitters to help, but it's not the same at all."

Yes, I know she has baby-sitters, Cassidy

thought, feeling sick. One baby-sitter in particular. My friend. My roommate. My friend and roommate who has easy access to that black TransAm. And maybe I still wouldn't suspect her, in spite of that, if it weren't for one other little thing. No, not so little. My friend and roommate had to have known all along that such a car was sitting in Professor Brenham's garage. But she never told me that even when I thought I was going insane because of a phantom car that looked exactly like it.

How could you baby-sit repeatedly for a family and not know they had a black TransAm sitting unused in their garage?

Yes, Cassidy thought, I know Leona Brenham has baby-sitters.

And one of them is Ann Ataska, my friend and roommate.

The medication was taking hold fully, turning Cassidy's limbs to water, making her eyelids heavy. But she couldn't sleep now. Not now, when she was so close to the truth.

The TransAm wasn't the only thing Ann had access to. The clock, the wristwatch, the invitation, the essay, the fanny pack with the money in it. At some point, Ann had had access to all of those things. She could have stolen Cassidy's letter to Misstery, destroyed it, and then written the phony letter of confirmation from the group. She hadn't been at the car wash, working, so she could have been at the car wash *driving the TransAm*. She'd been at the party at Nightmare Hall, and could have put coffee in a Coke can and a sticker on the cellar door. Cassidy remembered now how Ann had made such a big deal of the stickers at the party.

Ann.

Ann had been doing these things to her, making her feel like she'd fallen through the looking glass, and pretending all along that she was concerned?

Why? Why would Ann do this?

The telephone rang in the outer office.

"Be right back," Dr. Mandini said. "Don't go anywhere," she added, and laughed.

But I have to, Cassidy thought, struggling to sit up. I can't stay here, in this bed, when I have things to do. Important things. I have to find my dear friend and roommate and find out why she's making me crazy.

What was more important than finding out why someone was stealing your sanity? Your precious, valuable, absolutely essential mind?

When she slid off the table and tried to stand up, her legs folded underneath her as if they were made of paper. But she forced herself upright again, clinging to the edge of the bed. Grateful that she was still fully dressed, but wishing they'd left her boots on, she grabbed her purse from a chair beside the bed, let go of the table and struck out across the cold white tile in her bare feet, weaving unsteadily as she went.

The infirmary was so quiet, so deserted, except for the doctor, standing at the telephone with her back to Cassidy's cubicle. There was no sign of the other doctor.

I'm not insane, I'm not insane, Cassidy sing-songed jubilantly under her breath as she padded quietly, drunkenly, out of the room, down the hall, and out a side door. I'm as sane as anyone. It's a miracle, a miracle!

No, it's not, you silly twit, she reminded herself. You were never insane in the first place, so it's not a miracle at all.

Well, it felt like one.

The sidewalk outside the infirmary was icy-cold on her bare feet. Won't do to catch a cold now, she thought giddily, can't get sick, have things to do. Big things. Unmasking a criminal. Ann *was* a criminal. A mind is a terrible thing to steal.

It seemed to her as she slowly, unsteadily, made her way toward the Quad, looming in the distance, that campus had never looked more beautiful. The old-fashioned globes on poles lining the walkways provided a warm, soft glow, and there were enough leaves left on the huge old trees to give her some shelter from a thin, chilly drizzle that had begun to fall.

She wrapped her arms around her chest for warmth and murmured softly, "Now that I know my brain isn't rotting, I guess I love campus again. I guess I love just about everything again." Then she added angrily, clutching at a park bench for support as she passed it, "Except Ann. I don't love Ann. Not anymore."

It seemed to her that there was something more she was supposed to figure out, but she couldn't think what it was. Oh, yes . . . the why of it. Why would Ann, who had been her friend since day one on campus, do this terrible thing to her?

Travis? Was it because of Travis?

But that was very confusing, because Travis had kissed off Cassidy Kirk for good, hadn't he? So what was Ann worried about?

Idon'tknowIdon'tknowIdon'tknow, Cassidy thought as she stumbled over a fire hydrant and nearly fell to her knees.

"Watch where you're going!" she told the hydrant, and was thinking how far away the Quad still seemed to be when a car pulled up a few feet from her and parked. A tall figure in white jumped out and began running toward her.

"There you are!" a voice called, and Cassidy halted, curious. Of course here I am, she thought, watching as the figure approached, where else would I be? "Dr. Mandini has been looking all over for you! What in heaven's name do you think you're doing, young lady?"

Cassidy tried to focus her fuzzy vision. Someone tall, all dressed in white, was running up to her. White mask over the lower half of its face, a white surgical cap over its hair. A doctor, coming toward her.

Cassidy peered at the white jacket when it arrived at her side. A plastic tag pinned there read, *"Dr. Robert Caswell, M.D."*

"You are Cassidy Kirk, are you not?" a deep voice said in annoyance.

Cassidy nodded. The tone of voice told her she should probably feel guilty, but she wasn't sure why. Why was he mad at her?

"I want you to know, young lady," the doctor said, "that I was about to stitch up a severely lacerated forearm when Dr. Mandini came running in and told me you'd taken off on us. You've been medicated, and you have no business roaming around campus. Now, come with me."

"I'm not roaming," Cassidy said indignantly.

"I'm going back to my room. To find Ann. If you ask me, *she's* the one you should be yelling at, not me. I haven't done anything wrong, but *she* has."

But he had already taken her elbow and was leading her back to his car. She didn't have the strength to resist. Maybe, once they were in the car, she could talk him into just dropping her off at the Quad. She was awfully sleepy. Maybe she'd have to wait until tomorrow to do whatever it was she was supposed to be doing. Something about Ann . . . Ann Ataska, her dear friend and roommate . . . what was it?

"You young people!" the doctor said in an exasperated voice, "never a thought for anyone but yourselves. Upsetting the whole infirmary, taking me away from my patient, it's disgraceful."

"You're not as nice as the other doctor," Cassidy announced loudly. "I like her better."

And then they were at the parked car and Cassidy looked over at it and there was something about it, something that chilled her blood, something really, really wrong . . .

Black, tinted windows, and there they were, the two dangling hearts on the door.

Couldn't be, couldn't, couldn't. Because there was something in her cottony mind about the doctor who owned the TransAm being dead, dead for a whole year, and didn't she already know that there wasn't another car like it anywhere on campus? This car was supposed to be safely parked in a garage.

"This is *not* your car!" she said in a haughty voice, pulling away from the hand on her elbow, "and I'm *not* riding in a stolen car!"

Then it was too late, because the rough voice said, "Oh, yes, you are!" and grabbed her elbow more tightly and pushed her not into the front seat or the backseat, but around to the back of the car. A hand reached out and lifted the open trunk lid, another hand pushed hard on the small of Cassidy's back, shoving her into the yawning space. She cried out, but she was already toppling forward, into the trunk. She landed, facedown, on rough, moldy-smelling carpet.

She cried out again as the lid slammed shut. And then she was alone in the closed trunk of the TransAm.

Chapter 22

Stunned, Cassidy lay with her cheek against the rough carpet as the car began moving. She fought fiercely to think, but her head was spinning. Not a doctor, he wasn't a doctor, he couldn't be, he had only pretended to be. And this wasn't his car. How had he taken it from Professor Benham's garage?

Where were they going? Was the car leaving campus? It seemed to be moving very slowly.

Probably doesn't want to get a ticket, Cassidy thought, trying desperately to clear her head. I am a prisoner in the trunk of a car being driven by a fine, upstanding citizen who avoids traffic tickets . . . but has nothing against kidnapping.

Prisoner. She was a prisoner? And the smell in her prison was beginning to get to her. Moldy. Airless. Not good for her. Not good at all.

Think, think! she urged her brain. Now that you know you haven't lost your mind, never *were* losing it, you can figure a way out of this mess. But you have to think!

Her chest was already beginning to ache. Reaching down beside her for her shoulder bag, she felt nothing. Her fingers clutched, searched, but it wasn't there. Oh, no! He must have grabbed it from her before he closed the trunk lid. The purse, and her precious inhaler, were gone.

She couldn't see a thing, but she began feeling around with her hands. There, a pile of something soft and damp, with a strong mildewy smell. Towels? Wet towels?

Cassidy sagged back against the spare tire well. Those towels weren't the result of a gym workout. Someone who knew her well, knew she was severely allergic to mold and mildew, had deliberately put those towels in the trunk. In only minutes, she would be wheezing and coughing. And she didn't have her inhaler.

She struggled upward again and used her hands to search the trunk. There had to be something . . . her fingers touched something small and wooden. A handle? Smooth, worn. Her hand moved along its short surface, touching metal when it reached the end. A metal plate . . . a garden tool . . . something to dig with? Beside it, a cylindrical metal can . . . insecticide? . . . and a half-empty bag of what felt like dirt.

Garden supplies.

Cassidy struggled to remember what Dr. Mandini had said about the owner of the car. "He grows the most beautiful roses in this county."

There were other things in the trunk, rope, a small pile of newspapers, an old jacket that Cassidy wrapped around her for warmth. But she kept one hand on the garden tool with the short wooden handle, and the other on the can of what she hoped was insecticide.

She had already started to wheeze. The wet towels were getting to her. and there had to be a ton of dust, another allergen that gave her serious problems, in the trunk of a seldom-used car.

She had to get out of this trunk.

The car came to an abrupt halt.

Cassidy waited, gripping the garden tool and the can, for the trunk to open.

It didn't. It remained closed. But a moment later, a muffled voice called, "Cassidy? You in there?" and laughed softly. "Like, where else would you be, right?"

Cassidy didn't recognize the voice. She was beginning to wheeze, and calling out to the voice was going to take precious energy.

"Not dead yet?" the voice said. Cassidy could picture a head bent toward the trunk, mouth close to the metal lid. "Talk to me, if you can, so I'll know if I have to keep driving around. Waste of gas if you're already done for."

"Let me out!" Cassidy called, her lungs straining when she spoke. The wheezing was growing worse. She kicked the pile of towels into a far corner, knowing that wouldn't help.

"Can't do that. Letting air into your little corner of the world would defeat my purpose. But that awful sound you're making, trying to breathe, is nice to hear. Honestly, Cassidy, that is just about the worst noise I have ever heard! But it means that it won't be that long before you take your last breath, right? Maybe I'll even have time for a quick, healthy jog after I take the car back."

Cassidy crawled over to the edge of the trunk and slammed the can in her hand against the inside of the lid. "Please," she croaked, "please, I need my inhaler!"

Then, to her amazement, a key turned in the lock, and the lid lifted, only a few inches, but enough to send a whiff of cool, fresh air drifting into the trunk. Cassidy gulped it in gratefully. It helped a little.

A moment later, the plastic inhaler appeared in front of her, close enough to see, but not close enough to grab. "You mean this?" the voice taunted. "Is this what you need, Cassidy? Well, I'm sorry, but that's impossible. It would save your life, and that's not exactly what I had in mind."

"I . . . need . . . that . . . inhaler!" Cassidy muttered. The trunk lid was only open a few inches. Her captor was obviously holding it in place. But it wasn't tied and it wasn't chained. It was now or never, before the trunk lid slammed shut again, this time permanently.

Her lungs ached and the wheezing had grown worse, but Cassidy threw herself onto her back, lifted her legs with great effort and kicked upward with as much force as she could muster, sending the lid flying open all the way.

There was an exclamation of surprise from outside the trunk. In a voice no longer disguised, Cassidy's tormentor shouted, "You weren't supposed to have enough energy to do that!"

Even before Cassidy peered out of the trunk, she knew who the voice belonged to. She had heard it often enough.

So, when hands reached up to untie the

white mask and let it fall, and slip the white cap off the mass of golden hair that tumbled to the strong, healthy shoulders of an athlete, Cassidy was not the least bit surprised to see Talia Quick's enraged face staring down at her.

Chapter 23

"You?" Cassidy asked as Talia stared down at her. "I thought it was Ann." But everything that she had thought about Ann applied to Talia, as well, she realized quickly. Except . . . except for the car. "You were one of the students Professor Benham hired to drive her car? To keep it running?"

"I made a copy of the key the first time I drove the car. And I told her I'd come around and take it for a spin whenever I could. She's hardly ever home. Doesn't even know it's gone half the time." Talia sat down on the edge of the trunk, shaking her hair back into place. "I've kept it overnight twice, and she never said a word. She has her own car." Her rage gone, Talia talked as if they were having an ordinary, everyday conversation. Cassidy's painful wheezing deepened, and the sight of the inhaler clutched in Talia's hand filled her with

233

renewed desperation. It was so close, but she knew if she lunged for it, Talia would slam the trunk lid down. "What did you do with my bike? And where did you get its twin? And why didn't you pass Travis? Why didn't he see you?"

"I came back after you trotted off down the road. Put the twin, which I found through the Twin Falls classifieds, and then did make some minor adjustments to, on the road, and stuck yours in the trunk. It's resting comfortably in the old quarry at the state park. And Travis didn't see me, because I didn't pass him. There's a cutoff just before you get to that second curve."

Struggling to draw every single breath, Cassidy gasped, "But you were with Sophie at the mall that day . . . helping her pick out a dress for the dance."

"No, I wasn't. If you'd been listening on the shuttle afterward, you'd have heard Sophie boast that she picked out her dress all by herself. She was so pleased, but you didn't even hear her. We separated right after you left. I'd already parked the car behind the mall that morning and taken the shuttle back to campus. After we played our little game, I drove the car around behind the mall, parked it again, and met Sophie at the sporting-goods store where she thought I'd been shopping. Later that night, when everyone was asleep, I just hopped the shuttle again to the mall and brought the car back to campus."

Cassidy felt dizzy. Her lungs weren't providing enough oxygen to her brain. She could pass out at any time. "What did I hit on the road near Nightmare Hall?"

"Malcolm."

"Malcolm?"

"Sophie's stuffed, life-size alligator. Don't worry, though, Cassidy, there's hardly a scratch on him. You didn't hit him very hard. He's back in his chair in our room, where he belongs."

Between coughing spasms, Cassidy managed, "You were deliberately trying to make me think I was losing my mind. Why, Talia? I don't understand."

"I couldn't help it, Cassidy. I needed to see what it would take to drive a really strong mind insane. It was very important to me. I picked you because I knew you had that kind of mind." Talia began swinging the inhaler absentmindedly, back and forth, back and forth.

The sight of her lifesaving medication, so close and yet so unattainable, was maddening to Cassidy. "That's crazy," she gasped, clutching the can in her hand more tightly. "Why didn't you just ask your mother? She knows all that stuff."

Talia threw her head back and laughed, loud and wildly. "My mother? My *mother*? My mother isn't a *doctor*. My mother is a *patient*. Has been for years. In that same prestigious hospital where you all believed she was on the staff." Talia laughed again. "On the staff. That's so funny. Don't you think that's funny, Cassidy?"

"Your mother is . . . your mother is a mental patient? But . . . but you said I could call her, ask her for advice."

Talia laughed again. "My mother couldn't give advice to the baskets she weaves. But I knew you'd never call her. People like you never ask for help. You're so busy proving how strong and independent you are, you can't bear to hand that control over to someone else."

Travis had hinted at the same thing.

"I meant it when I said I understood how you felt, being laughed at," Talia said. "I was ten when my mother ran out of the house one day in her slip and bare feet and tried to hang herself from a tree in the front yard. Half the town saw her before she was taken away." Talia's voice grew bitter. "Ten-year-olds think that kind of thing is very funny. They never let me forget it. I decided then that I would study the mind when I grew up."

"But . . . but you said she was a *doctor*," Cassidy accused.

"When I got here, and all the rest of you had relatives working in the field of psychiatry, I decided to promote my mother from patient to doctor. I get letters from the hospital, updating me on her condition, so I figured it would be easy to pretend. And it was."

Cassidy could no longer sit up. She sank back again against the tire well. They were, she had realized, parked behind the infirmary on campus. Why couldn't someone in there hear the horribly loud, agonized sounds she was making? Dr. Mandini would know what they were. She would recognize the sound and come running, wouldn't she?

"My father," Talia said in that same conversational tone of voice, "said my mother lost her mind because she was weak. I didn't believe him. That's a horrible thing to tell a little girl, that her own mother is weak. I needed to prove him wrong. I've always needed that, more than anything. And if you had fallen apart the way I wanted you to, you would have proved him wrong for me. You would have proved that she wasn't weak, after all, that even a strong person can have a mental breakdown. But you didn't prove my father wrong, Cassidy, and I can't forgive you for that. I *hate* you for it, and I'll never forgive you."

"Yes, I did, Talia," Cassidy gasped, "I did prove your father wrong! You *did* drive me over the edge. I was hysterical when Jess and Ian took me to the infirmary. But then Dr. Mandini told me there really was a TransAm, and I knew I hadn't imagined things, so . . ."

Talia's face filled with rage again. "Stop lying! It didn't work, my father was right, and I hate you for that. I don't need you anymore. No one needs you, Cassidy, so I'm going to close the trunk now and leave. When I come back, in a couple of hours, you'll be dead. I'll take you out of the trunk, prop you under a tree, and take this car back to its owner. You won't have your inhaler when they find you. Everyone will know you left the infirmary because you were too rattled to know what you were doing, you had an attack, and without your inhaler, you died. There won't be any questions."

Red-and-orange spots began to dance before Cassidy's eyes. She knew she had very little time left.

"I'm not weak like my mother," Talia said, standing up. "I'm strong. I have to work very hard at it, but I'm going to succeed. I'm never going to be like her, never!"

"I . . . think . . . you . . . are," Cassidy whispered weakly between agonized spasms. "I . . . think . . . your . . . mother's . . . illness . . . is . . . hereditary. You're . . . as . . . sick . . . as . . . she . . . is."

The transformation in Talia then was terrifying. Her face contorted with fury. There was no vestige left of the calm, cool, smiling Talia of moments before. "That's not true!" she screamed, leaning over the open trunk. "How dare you say such a thing? You take that back! It's not true! I'm not like her, I'm not!"

The life-saving inhaler was only inches away from Cassidy. But she refused to let go of the can or the garden tool. She needed them even more.

"I wish I could watch you," Talia hissed. "I wish I could stay here and drill a hole in the trunk and just watch every second of your struggle to breathe. I want to see your eyes bulge out and your lips turn blue and know that those lips will never be able to tell anyone the truth about me or my mother."

"Yes, they will," Cassidy gasped, and she brought the can up and pushed down on the little white button at the top, praying that the can wasn't empty.

It wasn't.

A fine spray of foul-smelling chemicals hit

Talia full in the face. She screamed, her hands flying to her eyes, and Cassidy raised the garden tool and swung. It was a weak swing as she struggled for breath, but the metal tip caught Talia just above the temple. She toppled sideways like a felled tree.

To the sound of the hoarse croaks escaping from between her lips, Cassidy crawled out of the trunk. She scooped up the inhaler and pressed it to her mouth.

She was bending to see if Talia was breathing when a figure came running from the infirmary, shouting, "What's going on out there?"

Cassidy breathed a sigh of relief when she realized it was Dr. Mandini.

"What are you doing out here?" the doctor asked, hurrying toward her, not close enough yet to see Talia lying on the ground. "That was strong medication I gave you. You shouldn't be walking around. Are you crazy?"

"No," Cassidy said, in a strong, clear voice, "I'm not."

Epilogue

The rec center looked exactly as Cassidy had pictured it in her mind. The round tables were covered with floor-length black velvet cloths, and there were silver candlesticks in the center of each table, mated with a silver bud vase housing a single red carnation. More silver candlesticks stood on shelves and on tables near the bandstand, turning the plain, square room into a softly-glowing fantasyland.

"You were right about the black and silver," Sophie told Cassidy warmly. "It's perfect." Sophie looked adorable in the pale blue dress she had picked out by herself.

Cassidy smiled at her. "It is, isn't it? Well, if you ask me, it's about time something was perfect."

Ann passed by with her date, her face pale and lovely and expressionless. She nodded at Cassidy and Sophie. Cassidy returned the nod without a smile. It was still hard to believe that Ann hadn't known about the existence of the TransAm. She had told all of them that she had never gone into the garage and Professor Benham had never mentioned the car. She had said that she never saw Talia come for the car. That Talia had only come when Ann had taken the children to the park or to a movie. That she had absolutely no idea the car even existed.

Maybe. But it had seemed to Cassidy that she had seen something in Ann's eyes, something that said she wasn't telling the complete, unvarnished truth.

Travis must have seen it, too. He had called Cassidy the day after Talia had been taken away. They had talked for hours. She had agreed to slow down a little, now that she had already proved how strong she really was, and he had agreed to let her set her own pace.

"When I have my own house," Cassidy said as Travis took her hand and led her out onto the dance floor, "I'm not even going to use electric lights. Only candles."

"Cost you a fortune in fire insurance," he said.

"Oh, you're such a romantic," she said, but she smiled as she said it.

"Great dance, Cassidy!" Sawyer called out as he danced by with his date. "You did a terrific job, as always."

"Yes," she said, not at all out of breath from dancing, "I did, didn't I?"

About the Author

"Writing tales of horror makes it hard to convince people that I'm a nice, gentle person," says **Diane Hoh**.

"So what's a nice woman like me doing scaring people?

"Discovering the fearful side of life: what makes the heart pound, the adrenaline flow, the breath catch in the throat. And hoping always that the reader is having a frightfully good time, too."

Diane Hoh grew up in Warren, Pennsylvania. Since then, she has lived in New York, Colorado, and North Carolina, before settling in Austin, Texas. "Reading and writing take up most of my life," says Hoh, "along with family, music, and gardening." Her other horror novels include *Funhouse*, *The Accident*, *The Invitation*, *The Fever*, and *The Train*.

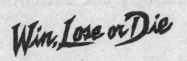

Win, Lose or Die

I watch her racing around the tennis courts, and I can't stand the sight of her.

She took something from me. She stole from me.

Oh, it wasn't an ordinary theft. Not the kind where you call the police and fill out forms for the district attorney and attend the trial of the criminal who ripped you off.

This was a different kind of theft. No police, no D.A., no trial. She was never seen punished.

She took something that I needed, and then she went blithely on with her life, as if nothing had happened.

I went on with mine, too. Got up every morning. Brushed my teeth and my hair, put on my shoes, ate, talked, did what I was supposed to do, slept. As if nothing had happened, just like her.

But something *had* happened. Something outrageous. An injustice.

Of course, I can't leave it this way. It's not right. It's just not right.

To balance the scales, I must take something from her.

I must take something that she can't run right out and replace, as if she'd simply lost her wallet or her keys or a pen.

There is only one thing that I can take from her that's completely irreplaceable.

Her life.

And that is what I'm going to take.

THRILLERS